I0679102

THE PASSENGERS

A SUSPENSE NOVEL

Charles Eric Jambor

To Erika with all my love. It was a "good call".

To Dr. David Szalay for another lease on life.

Publisher note: This is a work by Charles Eric Jambor. All
individuals and events have been invented and seen through
the personal life of Charles Eric Jambor.

"The Passengers" may be ordered by e-mailing Charles Eric
Jambor directly: yardmarx@nornet.on.ca
The book is also available from Amazon and at BJ-s in Simcoe.

Published by Karoly-J Ltd. Publishing.

Library and Archives Canada Cataloguing in Publication

Jambor, Charles E. (Charles Eric), author.
The Passengers/ Charles Eric Jambor
Issued in print and electronic format
ISBN 978-0-9940881-1-6 (ppk)

Charles Eric Jambor

Brantford Train Station.

REVIEWS

"I enjoyed the journey. Quite a suspense novel.
It is certainly a publicity stunt never thought of before.
Maybe you should write for movies."
Anne Sauve.

*****

"What can authorities do if people are abducted and there is no ransom demand?
While the story starts with a mystery, it ends with an unexpected surprise."
Bernard Crawshaw.

*****

"One can never be sure of what the future holds...
'Passengers' is a prime example of the twists and turns of life!
Impressive, intriguing and captivating."
Jim Koshowski.

*****

"This is not an ordinary suspense novel.
This story will keep you awake at night and make you think;
is this at all possible? ...Then you answer yourself; yes it is possible."
Marg Keller.

*****

"A stunning example of a gripping storey told in two hundred pages, not in five hundred."

*****

"An unexpected shift of loyalty and painful realization of how life can change in a minute."

*****

"Mr. Jambor is a late bloomer but that's okay. I understand he has another thriller in the works; "Devotedly yours. I wonder what that one is about?"

PREFACE

McCall never wanted to be a policeman because he couldn't see himself hiding behind some bushes and catching people speeding down the road. He thought that was a dastardly thing to do. Never the less he became a police officer by accident, twice!

Originally he was a golf equipment sales rep, living in the vibrant community of Myrtle Beach, South Carolina.

Since there was a golf course on almost every block, he joined the Myrtle Beach National and did most of his 'sales pitches' there. Not long after he became a member, he met and befriended the local Sheriff, who at the time was ready to retire.

They were sitting at a table one day having a few beer when the conversation turned to drugs and dealers. They both agreed crime was getting out of hand.

McCall looked at the Sheriff and asked him if there was anything he could do to help remedy the situation.

"If you think you're so smart, pass the required test in law enforcement and I'll make you my deputy and you can clean this town up."

McCall must have wanted the job bad enough because he studied and passed the test and accepted the Sheriff's offer. Within a year he had gotten rid of the drug dealers and at election time, he became the Sheriff for the next two years. To him, it was the most boring job he'd ever had.

When the two years were up he quit and returned to his roots in Canada and joined the Heron Point Golf and Country Club in Ancaster, Ontario. The land used to belong to his family.

When Hamilton's chief of police, who also belonged to the club, found out that McCall was a former Sheriff in South Carolina, he hired him on the spot. McCall quickly rose in the ranks and became the superintendent.

The rest of this amazing story will unfold as you read on. Most of the locations are real.

CHAPTER 1

Heron Point Golf and Country Club in Ancaster is one of the most prestigious clubs in Ontario and was lucky to have both the police Chief Dennis Stewart and the police Superintendent Chance McCall among its membership. The club also had Lucas Wilson, a world renowned magician/illusionist, John Edmonds, Edmonds Inc. Insurance Adjusters of North America and Brad Smith, a popular insurance company owner as members.

While Stewart and his wife Margaret were laid back, golfing whenever they felt like it, the four guys were fiercely competitive. They were often involved in charitable events. When they played together, it was mostly McCall and Lucas against John and Brad. They played for small amounts of money. Just enough to make every shot count.

McCall had arranged a game for Monday, with a 9:46am tee off time. He called Wilson's house, but there was no one home so he left a message on the answering machine.
Normally McCall would have finished work at 4:30pm this Friday, but instead he had been busy all day and into the early evening with a delicate domestic case that he had wanted to handle himself. This was especially poor timing for McCall because he was to start his vacation right after work.

The situation resolved, he went back to his office, cleared his desk and switched his mind to golf and to his vacation with his girlfriend, Lorraine Wilkinson. She was going to drive her car to his apartment in Toronto and on Monday they were going to Port Dover, Lorraine driving her car and he his motor bike. The Greater Hamilton Police Department would have to do without him until he returned, he thought. Just to be on the safe side, he phoned Lucas again to verify the tee off time. Lucas' wife Missy picked up the phone. "Hey, waz up, captain?" Missy called McCall captain because it was easier than his official title of superintendent.

"Hey Missy, is Lucas there?"

"He's at a meeting right now and we'll be on stage at the Niagara Casino in a few hours. We have a gig on Saturday too, at the Blue Mountain resort. You want him to call you... he knows about the tee off time."

"Oh, I just wanted to be sure we had a foursome for Monday."

"Yes, he talked to both Brad and John, and they are okay."

"Then he doesn't have to call me back. See you."

"Love you captain." "Love you too, Missy. Bye.

McCall rode his Harley to every Friday the Thirteenth in Port Dover, summer or winter. This year there was only one Friday the Thirteenth and it was in June which was next week. McCall usually took three of his six-week vacation in the summer, saving the other three weeks for the winter when he and Lorraine would go golfing and snorkeling on some exotic island in the south. Lorraine had told him she would have everything planned out including Friday the Thirteenth. McCall left the planning to her because she was good at it and he contended women were better at planning vacations anyway. The only thing he arranged himself was the golf games. He glanced out the window and saw some clouds blocking the sun. But the outdoor thermometer on the window frame still read 26C for the third day now. He liked it even warmer. At his office he fought with everyone over the temperature but mostly the women because they had to have the air conditioner set at 18C max. Generally he kept his office door shut and the window cracked open.

Now that he had calmed down the jealous husband in that domestic incident, he was relieved that nobody had gotten hurt or been sent to jail and he was anxious to get out of the office. He was in a good mood. He was closing the window when his phone rang. It was the desk sergeant. He stated there was a hysterical person on the 911 line yelling something about a train derailment in Brantford and someone should talk to him. McCall said he would, and pushed the lit button. After identifying himself, he listened to the man's frantic rant about a bus load of passengers that had gone missing from the Western Rail Lines (WRL) station in Brantford. The man's name was Ed Clement.

McCall didn't know it, but this phone call would change his life forever.

Stunned, he hung up and started to digest what he had just heard. The disappearance of a busload of WRL passengers from a decommissioned railroad station in Brantford didn't make any sense. He had jotted down Clement's number, and modified the story slightly to make it more believable. He immediately called Chief Stewart at home because he was going on vacation, and by the sound of things, this case would require prompt attention.

~

Chief Stewart was a cigar smoking man. Even though he wasn't supposed to smoke at the station, he smoked in his own office and sometimes when he got overly excited he would walk smoking into the general office area. He usually kept the cigar in his mouth and talked around it. But when McCall phoned him and told him about the WRL passengers disappearance, he took the cigar out of his mouth and in a clear voice he asked, "Did you have some bad drugs today, McCall?"
McCall replied that he didn't, he wasn't on any medication and he

was getting ready to leave on his vacation.

"You say a bus full of people has gone missing, just like that?"

To help the chief understand better, McCall repeated the story very slowly from the beginning.

"Okay chief... apparently this Master Panel Operator (MPO) phoned Ed Clement, a former railroad employee, at his home. Clement is now the caretaker at the decommissioned Brantford train station. You know the old TH&B station in Brantford?"

"Yeah...?"

"Well, the MPO told Clement there was a freight derailment at Two Mile Bridge just east of Brantford. He asked Clement to open up the station at 6:30pm and let the passengers wait there until transfer buses arrived. Eager to help his old employer out, he told the MPO he'd be happy to do that and would be on his way immediately. He went to the station and opened it up. Clement said at 6:35 the train arrived and all the passengers got off and he took them inside the building. He then started showing them some of the old posters on the walls, the spittoons, the pot-bellied stove, you know... history. And in a few minutes at 6:45 or so, a bus pulled up. The driver waved to Clement, loaded up his bus and drove away. Everybody else was left waiting for the rest of the buses, but no more buses showed up."

"This is too bizarre, McCall," the chief cut in, chewing on his cigar now. "How come this Clement guy called us and not the MPO or whomever? And what did he use for a phone if the station was decommissioned?"

"He called the railroad head office using his cell phone, but they couldn't tell him anything because they hadn't heard about the derailment yet. That's when Clement decided to call 911 because he had to get an answer. He was really shaken up."

"This has got to be a hoax... this is unbelievable."

"It is, chief," McCall agreed and continued explaining.

12

"You see, the train engineer William Bertling, couldn't call the MPO on his communication radio because there was bad static on the line and he couldn't use the rail phone either because of the derailment."

"Is this for real?" the chief cut in again.

"I know, chief. Anyway, after the remaining passengers were all left waiting at the old train station ten to fifteen minutes or so, this engineer Bertling, got really worried and borrowed a cell phone to call the head office in Toronto. That's when all holy hell broke loose. There was no derailment anywhere. It was only a broken tab on the rail, possibly near Two Mile Bridge. That broken tab put the signals and the rail phone out of service. Clement was totally hysterical. I thought I'd better let you in on this, chief, because something has to be done and you know I'm going on vacation."

McCall mentioned his vacation again, hoping it would sink in. There was a long silence and in the background he could hear some hollering and some kids screaming. Then he heard splashing sounds that undoubtedly came from the chief's swimming pool.

"So, this is not a joke, eh?" The chief said sort of to himself and again with the cigar in his mouth. McCall assured him this wasn't a joke. There was more silence. As the chief was thinking, he was looking past the sizzling steaks on his barbeque and saw his twelve year old nephew who, despite the large "NO RUNNING" sign, was chasing his nine-year old sister. Then he looked at the kid's father, Adam, his wife's younger brother, sprawled out in a plastic dinghy. Narrowing his eyes, he stared for a moment at the obese man and decided he wasn't going to fix his 140 dollar speeding ticket, even if his wife would never speak to him again. Looking away from the pool and blending a mouthful of cigar smoke with the smoke rising from the barbeque, he asked McCall, "Where is the train now?"

"The train is in Brantford at the old station," McCall said.

"Okay, you call that caretaker, what's his name, Clement and tell him to hold the train there and not to leave the station.

13

Then call the Brantford OPP, (Ontario Provincial Police) and
have someone get the names and addresses of the remaining
passengers. Then get WRL on the phone and tell them I want to
talk to them and I'll be in my office in fifteen minutes. Whoever is
in charge in Brantford, tell them to hold off the media on this
altogether. I'll do the talking from this end. Then you get in your
car and burn rubber all the way to Brantford."

McCall didn't like the situation at all and wanted to scream
at the chief that he was already into his vacation time and wanted
someone else to handle this case, but he was pretty certain he
would be fighting a battle he couldn't win. Swallowing some
unsavoury words, he looked up the Brantford OPP's number and
when he called, he learned that a Captain Rutherford was in
charge and the call was transferred to his home. Rutherford
agreed he would cooperate and would meet him at the station.
Then he got hold of Clement and advised him not to go home and
that he'd be there as soon as possible.

~

Captain Rutherford was a tall thickset man with a
pockmarked round face and had piercing eyes. His grey hair was
about the same length as the quills on a medium size porcupine
and protruded from his head the same way. When McCall got him
on the line he had no idea what McCall was talking about. Once
the situation was detailed to him, just like Chief Stewart,
Rutherford thought it was crazy. At the time McCall thought he
was going crazy too.
"How does your Department in Hamilton get involved in a
bizarre situation like this, that occurred in Brantford?" Rutherford
asked.
McCall wanted to tell him he didn't know, but changed his
mind and told him the truth. It was a long story and to make it
short, he just stated that the chief and himself had been talking to
the Rail Police a few months ago to discuss some union business.

Apparently, prior to 1998, the CN rail (Canadian National) service ended in Brantford. Now it ends in Hamilton. So Brantford is now in Hamilton's jurisdiction as far as the rail line is concerned. But Brantford is still in the 'old book'.

"Why are you asking? You want to handle this?" McCall asked Rutherford quickly and coyly.

"No, no. You're not going to get any argument from me. You can have it," Rutherford replied briskly.

"See ya in a little while then," McCall said, feeling sharp jolts of pain in his brain. He hung up and started thinking. What's happening? Has this got something to do with terrorism? Why are terrorists picking on Brantford? Brantford is a small city in comparison to New York, LA, or Madrid. The situation confounded him. On the way out to his car, he told the night sergeant he was going to Brantford and would be back shortly. The sergeant replied he'd be around and showed him an upturned thumb.

~

Driving to Brantford on HWY 403, McCall's mind was on the abducted passengers and he began to think that this had to be something big. He also thought about Lorraine and the places they might be going to tonight. Maybe they'd go to a disco or jazz bar. He liked jazz and Lorraine liked disco. She liked the sound of crisp paper money rattling through a counting machine the best. She talked shop a lot. She was head of the loans department at the Royal Chartered Bank of Canada (RCBC) in St. Thomas. Aside from the getting married and settling down part, McCall had no other issues with Lorraine. And when she started into discussing bank business, she always brought up examples, market trends and investment opportunities. Most of the time, he had no idea what the hell she was talking about. It amazed him how she remembered all those numbers and charts. And whenever she started hinting about backyards and front yards and pools, he had to change the subject.

15

*****

Lucas Wilson could remember numbers too. He and his wife Missy lived in a gorgeous house in Port Dover overlooking Silver Lake. They had a beautiful swimming pool in their yard. From there they could see all the way down to Long Point. He liked the Wilsons a lot. They were all around the same age. Lorraine and himself were 35; Lucas 38 and Missy 34. Lucas Wilson was an entertainer with many talents. Since he was ambidextrous he could write with both hands at the same time. With his left hand he could write his name the right way and with his right hand he'd write it backwards, in mirror image. He had a sharp memory too. He would blow people away with his antics. He could remember a deck of cards laid out in front of him in random order and could read a book two pages at a time and those two pages would take him only a few seconds. He'd memorize the page numbers and the text on the pages. If he wanted to, he could remember those pages forever. He could memorize a foreign book too, but he couldn't understand what he'd read. He was famous for elaborate magic tricks along with some simple ones. McCall had learned some of his simple tricks and used them on his family at special occasions. Wilson laughed when he told him this. But Wilson knew McCall was a better golfer than he was.

Whenever they went to a Friday the Thirteenth, McCall they would ride around Dover together. McCall, with Lorraine perched on the back of his Harley. Lucas would ride with Missy. Then McCall and Lucas would have a few beers in a bar, Lorraine and Missy would go shopping or looking at houses for sale. Lorraine was always planning to get married. But McCall figured otherwise. If push came to shove, he could be persuaded into living together.

~

With his unmarked cruiser, lights flashing, he was clicking one-hundred and fifty kilometres an hour and dreaming of birdies and pars. Suddenly, from out of nowhere, an elderly man cut in front of him. To avoid a collision he had to jam on the brakes and ended up skidding onto the left shoulder. He knew cops weren't supposed to show road rage, but when he caught up with the old man he screamed at him. The poor man apologized vehemently. McCall ended up feeling sorry for the old guy and let him go without a ticket.

In Brantford, as he turned off onto the Wayne Gretzky Parkway he had to think about what street he needed to take to get to the railroad station. He got to Grey Street and from there he ended up right in front of the old station. As he was getting out of his cruiser, he saw Captain Rutherford already waiting at the main entrance, with a cheerful look on his face.

"Hey Superintendent, I have some good news for you. We have a make on the bus. It's a regular tour bus that was signed out at a Simcoe depot by a licensed long distance driver. The bus plate number is BO4278 and the equipment number is 3864. I talked to the bus owner and he's all shook up. He thinks the driver gave him some false documents. He said when he dialled the number he was given, the phone just rang and rang and no one picked up. The driver's name apparently is Charles Parker, Caucasian, brown hair and wearing a grey uniform. He rented the bus for a week and paid cash."

"So where is this Parker guy from?" McCall asked just as... "unit five-zero-eight, come in please" crackled on his car radio.

"Hold on captain, I'll be with you in a minute," he said and jumped into his cruiser.

"This is five-zero-eight, Superintendent McCall."

"I have Chief Stewart for you, superintendent," said the female voice.

"Go ahead chief," McCall said.

"McCall, be sure to talk to the conductor and the engineer

17

before they take the train home and then get every detail you can from Ed Clement. This is freaky, McCall. No one seems to know anything. No one's heard from anyone. No one's come forward. I don't like this at all."

McCall promised he'd do his best and signed off. Then he got back to Rutherford.

"As I was saying, where is this Parker person from?"

"Actually, he's from Toronto. At least that's what it said on the copy of his driver's licence and he had a Toronto number. The owner also told me Parker came with two other guys that looked pretty decent to him," Rutherford said.

"We'll have to deal with those guys later," McCall said, and requested to see the conductor and the train engineer.

After the two pushed their way through a group of passengers, Rutherford lead McCall out to the conductor's confine which was part of the Post Office car. They walked by stacks of mail and
parcels before getting to the office. Both the conductor and the engineer were there. Rutherford introduced both men to McCall.

Kleiner the conductor, was a tall, stern-looking individual, whereas the engineer, William Bertling was a short chubby man in his late fifties. He wore the traditional striped cap and a red scarf. He had glasses and a gentle round face. McCall read him as an honest man but he wasn't too sure about Kleiner's virtues. Neither of the two men was in a very good mood. Captain Rutherford introduced McCall as the superintendent from the Greater Hamilton Police Detachment. McCall talked to Kleiner first, using a relaxed style of questioning. He indicated no one was being blamed and stated the true fact that the police had absolutely no knowledge as to whether this was an abduction or what. Somehow, he managed to put Kleiner at ease.

"Now, as for the actual instructions we received from the MPO..." Kleiner said as he pointed a finger in the direction of what appeared to be a black box beneath his Panasonic 240 radio, "It's all there. And by the way, you can verify this on Bill's receiver too," he said. Bertling was nodding while Kleiner pressed a playback button on the side of the radio. He waited a few seconds and then pressed the button again. After the sound of some static, a male voice came in crisp and clear:

"This is the MPO. Attention WRL four-twenty. Location check. Give me your position."

"One-three kilometres from Brantford, easterly."

"That's me talking to the MPO," Bertling said.

"Okay four-twenty. There's a freight derailment at Two Mile Bridge. Stop the train at the old TH&B station in Brantford. We have made contact with the former stationmaster, Ed Clement. He'll be waiting for you there. Unload your passengers in Brantford. Buses will transfer them to Union Station in Toronto. Do not tie up radio personnel because there's also a hazardous material spill at the derailment site. All channels are needed for emergencies. Acknowledge four-twenty, over."

"Stop consist at the old TH&B station in Brantford, over and out."

"Okay, skipper, stay close to your command. We'll call you within forty-five minutes. The MPO was talking to Bertling, or rather the imposter was talking to Bertling. There's no way we could tell the difference between the real MPO or this guy," Kleiner said apologetically, flashing his right palm towards the radio. McCall couldn't find anything wrong with the message either. The tape was still rolling when Kleiner motioned to McCall and said "Listen to this. Here I am trying to double check with headquarters on the rail phone and all I get is a steady buzz. That's a sign of a fractured rail. As the buzz intensified, the train was getting closer and closer to the derailment site."

"What would happen, say, if you hadn't heard a message

or Mr. Bertling had a heart attack?" McCall asked Kleiner.

"Well, two years ago the train would have run into the derailment. Today, though, it would stop short a mile or so from the mishap. Firstly, we have an automatic detection system, ADS that notices trouble ahead. Secondly, if Bill would leave his seat the train would slow and stop. We have a 'Dead Man's Switch' on the engine. If he passes out or releases the control handle for some reason, the train slows and stops. Anyway, in this case there was no doubt in our minds that there was a derailment. And as for the bus transfer... that's standard procedure." McCall nodded.

"You can get a copy of this recording from head office, ours is locked in," Kleiner said, pursing his lips. As they were leaving, McCall shook hands with Kleiner and Bertling and said he'd get a copy of the recording later. Then he asked Bertling if he'd mind taking him onto the locomotive.

Bertling was surprised but said, "Ya ya, sure. No problem."

Being an older person, Captain Rutherford didn't want to climb onto the locomotive and McCall had no problem with that. As Bertling opened the door to the engine room, the strong smell of diesel fuel stirred up his olfactory senses. He felt mildly intoxicated. All his life he had been crazy about diesel engines and the aroma of diesel fuel always turned him on. The clattering of the idling engine left him breathless. This was the first time in his life he had actually seen the inside of a diesel - electric locomotive. At that moment he felt he would do anything to trade jobs with Bertling.

"Lucky guy," he said looking at Bertling, admiringly. He petted the carbody as he stepped forward into the instrument room. Bertling smiled proudly as he seated himself in his comfortable arm chair and motioned to McCall to sit in the co-pilot seat beside him. McCall sat down and felt like a king. The control room reminded him of the cockpit of a 707 that he once had a chance to view. Except here of course, the number of instruments was only a small percentage of the instruments on a 707.

"MAX. SPEED 120 KM", said the painted sign above the windscreen.

McCall read the speed out loud and remarked, "That's pretty fast."

"One hundred and twenty kilometres an hour on this baby is equal to seven hundred kilometres an hour on a jet," Bertling said, smiling.

McCall had no doubt. Absent-mindedly, he peered through a side window and gazed for a moment at the sky line of downtown Brantford. Out of simple curiosity, he asked Bertling,

"When your headlights are on, how far ahead can you see?"

"Oh, I can increase the power of the headlights to a maximum of four settings. On an open straight run I can pick out a cow standing on the track a kilometre down. Plenty of time to stop if I can't scare the spots off her first with these multi-pitched, multi-toned Leslie Supertyphon S5D horns," he said as he showed McCall a panel with buttons and dials on it. McCall was genuinely amazed. But there was something in the MPO's message that bothered him.

"Can you rewind your tape for me? I'd like to hear the instructions you received from this mysterious guy on your system again," McCall asked engineer Bertling as his mind was racing, searching for a clue, any clue. Bertling acted miffed but did what McCall asked him to do. The taped message was exactly the same message as Clement's.

"So, the MPO doesn't use any codes in the conversation?"

"Not needed," Bertling said, showing his left palm to McCall.

"When the MPO calls us, he quotes our number and this baby is 420. He pointed to the large numbers above the "MAX. SPEED" sign.

"So, how... ah... can a conductor be called then?"

"A conductor doesn't usually get called."Bertling replied as he glanced at McCall over his glasses.

"When he does get called and he's not in his office, I can

21

get him on the two-way radio. My set is built into the dash right here," and he pointed to some more buttons on the instrument panel. Kleiner has a portable radio. He doesn't like to use it because he thinks it disturbs the passengers. The kids like the two-way radios though. Reminds them of police communication. You know all about that, eh?"

"Yeah," McCall said, but he wished the hell he didn't. At this time he still didn't have anything to communicate to his chief. Reluctantly he left the engine room. Had the circumstances been different, they would have had to pry him out of it.

As he got off the locomotive, Captain Rutherford came over and informed him that the remaining passengers were back on the train and their names and addresses had been catalogued and as far as he was concerned, the train could leave for Toronto. McCall asked him to hold the train a little bit longer as he wanted to talk to the old caretaker again. Rutherford shrugged and lead him into the old TH&B station waiting room. There they found Ed Clement in the middle of a gaggle of news-hawks. Somehow they must have gotten wind of this strange 'kidnapping' and were hungry for details. McCall told them they had to wait because he didn't have any information at this time.

"Hope to God Clement didn't say anything to the reporters," he remarked to Rutherford who assured McCall that he wouldn't have, because he had ordered him not to. McCall took his word for that.

Rutherford motioned to Clement who in turn pointed to the station-master's office at the far end of the waiting room. They entered the office and Clement followed in right after them. Rutherford introduced McCall to Clement, who shook his hand with a pained smile. In his younger days, Clement must have stood six-foot-two or taller but today he appeared less than that. This bizarre experience had aged him, and it showed. The wrinkles on his forehead were deep-set. His eyes lacked sparkle and his hair was unkempt. There was a heavy odour of mothballs permeating the office, no doubt coming from Clement's blue regulation uniform. McCall was allergic to mothballs so he stood as far away from him as he could. Had it not been for Clement's aromatic pipe smoke, he would have had to leave the room altogether. Clement sat down behind his old desk and offered McCall a seat. McCall sat down. Clement regarded McCall with a mournful expression and in a soft tone of voice asked him if he wanted to hear the whole story.

"Yeah, better hear it from the top," McCall said. as he pushed the chair a little bit farther away from Clement's desk.

"Well, first of all, you know what TH&B means? Clement asked. McCall shook his head.

"TH&B stands for Toronto, Hamilton and Buffalo. Although the route was extended to Windsor in 1978, the same year WRL purchased the company from CN and it became a crown corporation, the name was unchanged. The letters TH&B are more commonly referred to as 'To Hell and Back', which fits this scenario appropriately," Clement said as he sighed heavily and gave McCall a pained smile. McCall smiled back and sucked his teeth.

With another sigh Clement continued, "So, I am showing the passengers some old posters of ships sailing to foreign lands, warnings to young women travelling alone, old schedules, the pot-bellied stove and the spittoons, and I hear someone honking a horn, and then this tall, slim uniformed guy comes in."

"Did you say this guy came in while the horn was blowing?" McCall asked with interest.

"Um... no, after. Like right after. I looked at my watch and it was 6:45. I thought that was pretty good timing. These people would be out of here pretty fast. If you can imagine, this station was packed.

"Anyway, this bus driver comes in and waves to me and I hear him saying that he wants to take 30 people. Then he starts sending them out... but, ah forget it. I'm just imagining things."

"What is it? Just go on," McCall urged Clement, hoping for a lead, anything.

23

"Well, I kind of thought it was odd that he said thirty people and didn't take those near the exit door but he sort of selected them, screened them, before he sent them out to the bus. He didn't take people with kids and as I recall, he chose mainly younger folks."

"Go on," McCall interjected anxiously while an idea began to formulate in his mind. Ransom. He was certain of it. WRL, or the city, or someone, will get a call for a million bucks pretty soon. A sigh of relief left his lips and he actually felt happy. This case was turning out to be a cakewalk, he thought. Negotiations would take a little time, but there wouldn't be too much work for him, as far as he was concerned. He considered this incident a textbook case. Most of the work would be done by the chief and his office. Besides, this was the beginning of his three-week vacation.

"Oh yea...," he heard Clement go on. "The driver said three more buses were on the way."

McCall heard Clement's voice like it came from a far-away cavern and impatiently cut him off. He figured aside from the identity of the people on the bus, nothing more Clement could have told him would have been of importance anymore. And surely he didn't know the identity of those passengers. Consequently, further conversation with him was pointless. He advised Rutherford to release the train. Rutherford stepped outside of the office and relayed this direction to Bertling who was pacing anxiously by the office door. Rutherford was immediately mobbed by reporters but was able to avoid them by darting back into the office.

"They will kill us," he wailed as he raised his hands towards the ceiling.

"We have guns, they don't," McCall said, taking him seriously nonetheless. As he got up from his chair, he praised Clement for calling 911 so promptly and for his uncanny ability to recall every little detail. With an anguished grimace on his face, he bid Clement goodbye and told him not to say anything to anyone but immediately sensed he had asked too much.

As Rutherford and McCall entered the waiting room, they were bombarded with questions. All the newshounds howled at once. The two avoided prying questions as McCall told them they had to get their information from Chief Stewart. He told them if he heard anything from the abductors, they'd be the first to know. So far the police had heard nothing. As Rutherford saw McCall to his car, he gave him the elbow and said, "Ransom, eh?"

"Probably," McCall answered as he felt a headache coming on.

"We'll keep you informed, or you'll keep us informed, captain," McCall said getting into his car.

The train was leaving the TH&B station and the clacking sound of the wheels reminded him of his younger days when his mother and father used to take him to Windsor. He remembered how the monotonous clacking noise used to put him to sleep. He hadn't been on a train since. He was wide awake now, with all kinds of crazy ideas swirling around in his head.

CHAPTER 2

With mixed emotions, McCall was pondering his vacation. During his drive back to Hamilton he practised different ways to present his theory to his chief. Counting on his ability to manage difficult cases boosted his self-esteem. All he had to do was live up to that image. He envisioned himself sitting in his chair, relaying the events as they unfolded from Clement, the train crew and Rutherford. He pictured the chief sitting in front of him sipping coffee from a Styrofoam cup, listening to his brief but thorough report. He radioed ahead to his sergeant asking if he'd heard anything. He said there was nothing new. No one was taking responsibility for the abduction.

Walking quickly, he entered the police station and caught the chief at the water fountain. The two went into McCall's office. As McCall shut the door and turned, to his great surprise Chief Stewart was puffing nervously on his cigar and preparing to sit in his chair. McCall swallowed and quickly reworked his imagined plan. He was seriously concerned about his new rocker arm chair. It had never supported two hundred and fifty pounds before. He moved towards his desk and sat down in front of it, as if he were the visitor. A cloud of cigar smoke headed his way and he crouched to avoid it. He rubbed his eyes and after noisily clearing his throat he recounted everything he knew about the abduction. After a moment's thought, Chief Stewart agreed with the ransom theory. This time, McCall actually welcomed the second hand cigar smoke, even though to him, a non-smoker, it smelled like a burning rope and horse manure.

There was a knock at the door. McCall turned his head and watched Corporal Dale enter. Dale went straight to the chief and informed him that the phones were ringing off the hook and the media people were breaking down the door. Through his waterlogged pupils McCall glanced at the chief's raised eyebrows and his vacillating cigar. Chief Stewart thought for a moment, then looked at his watch. While sending an endless smoke signal towards the ceiling, he turned to Dale and said, "Tell the news crew I'll have a statement at 22:15."

"Yes sir. Can I leave the door open chief? It's stuffy in here," Dale mumbled as he left McCall's office not bothering to shut the door anyway. In his mind, McCall thanked him for that. He noticed a free line on the phone, grabbed it and quickly dialled his home number. There was no answer. She's not there yet he thought to himself.

"Who are you calling?" the chief asked.

"I'm calling my apartment," McCall answered.

"Guess you're not home, eh?" Chief Stewart said sarcastically as he belched eight cubic feet of smoke into McCall's face.

"I'm calling my girlfriend Lorraine Wilkinson. She's supposed to be at my place."

"I see," said Stewart as he got up from behind the desk.

"Make out your report and meet me in the conference room. I'll put something together for the media." He left the office and shut the door behind him. With one giant stride, McCall jumped to the door, tore it open and fanned the room with it until his arm got tired. The visible part of the smoke was gone but the putrid smell remained trapped in everything, stinking up the whole room. He thought about his vacation again, but knew his police duty came first. With a foul taste in his mouth, he started typing his report.

~

At 22:05 McCall saw the chief coming towards his office. He leapt from his chair and ran out to meet him. Even though he had a new cigar in his mouth, it was just as awful smelling as the old one.

"What do you think of this," the chief said as he fumbled some sheets of paper while walking towards McCall's office.

"I'll listen to it in the hall, or we can go into the conference room chief. The floor had just been polished," McCall lied pointing at his office. The lie worked. Chief Stewart hung his glasses on his nose and started to read:

"Ladies and gentlemen: Around 6:40pm today a person or persons unknown broke in on the railroad radio frequency and sent a message to a WRL train engineer. By cutting off the connecting tab on the railroad tracks, this disrupted secondary communication lines thus faking a derailment at Two Mile Bridge. They stopped the WRL train at the old TH&B station in Brantford and from that station a Caucasian male dressed as a bus driver abducted about thirty people whose identities we do not yet know. We suspect there are some special people among those kidnapped. The majority of the passengers will likely be released once demands have been met. This is all we can tell you at this time."

"So what do you think. Will they buy this?"

"There isn't much else we can tell them, right? They'll have to buy it," McCall replied.

"Okay then. You come with me but don't say anything. I'll handle the hounds."

McCall agreed and followed the chief into the conference room. The room was filled with noisy reporters who quieted down as soon as the two arrived. Chief Stewart greeted them and read his statement. When he finished talking, there were a million questions coming at him from every direction. It was impossible to understand even one. Questions were directed at McCall too, but as they had previously discussed, he had no comment. Some of the questions were connecting this kidnapping with the middle east situation and that was indeed food for thought.

As they were leaving the conference room, Chief Stewart grabbed McCall's arm and led him into his own office to discuss the possibility of terrorism in this kidnapping.

"That would make this a brand new ballgame," McCall remarked.

McCall's forehead broke out in a cold sweat as he realized that he was not going on his vacation now. No question about it, the abducted passengers came first. There was a knock at the chief's door and it opened instantly. Corporal Dale entered with two executives from WRL and two minutes later Dale returned with the mayor. McCall excused himself and headed to his office to call home again. There was still no answer. He couldn't imagine what had happened to his girlfriend because she had never broken a promise before. She was supposed to be at his place today and it was now 11:00pm. She must have run into some problems. He decided to give her another half an hour before calling again. As 11:30 approached, he broke away again to call his home, but there was still no answer. He started to become very concerned.

He returned to the chief's office and told him there was one more person missing. McCall could tell the chief wasn't amused. He wasn't amused for two reasons. Firstly, Corporal Dale had just entered the office with two men from the RCMP. Secondly, Mrs. Stewart wanted him on line four. He spoke with Mrs. Stewart first and told her not to wait up for him and no he didn't care if Adam and his family were never coming over again, and no he wasn't getting mad, and no he didn't know when he was coming home tonight. Then he attended to the two RCMP officers and McCall phoned home once more. After ten rings he hung up and phoned Lorraine's apartment in St. Thomas. There was no answer there either. Something quite serious must have happened preventing her from getting to his apartment and from calling him to leave a message. He had known Lorraine most of his life and he knew she would have called him by now if she had been able to. What if she had had a car accident was a thought that flashed through his mind.

In the meantime, the number of concerned officials had grown greatly and they too had moved into the conference room. It was quarter after twelve and there was still no word of any demands or any sign of the kidnappers. This was getting to be unbelievable. No one had called or come forward with anything. The entire provincial police force had been alerted and had been instructed to be on the lookout for the tour bus. There were cruisers driving up and down Highways 403, 402, 401, the QEW and all other major roads. Every tour bus was being stopped and checked for the abducted passengers.

No one had any idea that the 'Mystery Bus' was already at its destination, tucked away behind some bushy pine trees.

Missing person calls had been coming in all evening. Remarkably, eleven of the 'thirty' passengers had been identified. None of them were wealthy or holding any key social position. Not knowing who the abductors were or what their demands were or even where they were located gave investigators absolutely nothing to go on. Collectively, the concerned officials decided to break up their meeting to go home and wait until something happened.

As the group dispersed, McCall told Chief Stewart that he was going home to continue trying to locate his girlfriend. The chief replied. "By all means." In fact, he was packing it in too. He couldn't imagine how such a thing could be happening. And to top it all off no ransom demand. He, along with everybody else, thought there had to be more to this than met the eye. He needed some time to think everything through.

~

When McCall arrived at his Toronto apartment, he took the stairs to the second floor and unlocked the door. Just as he flicked on the lights the phone rang. He was startled as well as relieved. What a coincidence that his girlfriend should be calling just as he was walking through the door. Thank God everything is all right, he started thinking. It's no wonder she couldn't reach me because I haven't been home and all the lines have been jammed at the police station.

"Hi, honey," he bubbled happily into the phone. The hundred pound stone that had just been lifted off his chest when the phone rang, became a thousand pounds when, after a moment's silence, he heard the chief's burly voice objecting to such an unusual address. McCall didn't need to explain himself. Chief Stewart understood his predicament. Stewart told him to postpone his vacation. He already sensed that was coming. Furthermore, he was to be in his office no later than 8am to be a stand-in for Frank Adams the deputy chief, who had been taken to hospital a few minutes ago with a heart attack.

Wow, he thought... Frank had a heart attack...that's not good. This just further complicates things. Bye-bye vacation forever, for sure.

Any other time, Stewart's request would have been greatly appreciated but this time McCall wasn't enthused about it at all. He thanked the chief for the directive and made no further comment.

With a heavy heart he sat down and started phoning people he thought might know where Lorraine was. He checked with major OPP detachments and with hospitals from St. Thomas to

Toronto. All his inquiries were in vain. He was totally drained.
His thoughts turned to the abducted people. He couldn't
imagine what these people must have felt. They would have had
to spend the night on a bus. How would they have coped? What
would they have had to eat? Were they going to be terrorized,
killed? Who is this maniac? Who are these maniacs? McCall
thought. Who would take that many people and how much
money would they want? This is unreal. He lay on his bed with
his eyes wide open staring at the reflection of a neon sign on the
wall. He started to think about Frank. Tomorrow he would have
sat down with Frank who would have started analyzing this
abduction from the start.

"There's always a clue," Frank would say.

There were many clues alright. McCall just had to look at
them all. It was pointless to get Chief Stewart involved. Stewart
was an administrator. He knew what the head office wanted and
he delivered. He had surrounded himself with police officers who
respected him and made him look good. Now they had to really
produce. He had to produce. This abduction had to be solved.
He mulled the whole incident over again and concentrated on the
four things that stood out and kept punching him in the face. The
MPO's message, the severed tab on the rail line, the 'special'
passengers and the rented bus itself. All these were complicated
things requiring weeks of investigation and technical knowledge.
In order to carry on with the police investigation, WRL would
have to supply him with vital data concerning Clement and the
train crew. Until then he would just have to hang in there and wait
for their reports. If there was no ransom demand then nothing
made any sense, and everything would come to an abrupt
standstill. He undressed and crawled into bed.

His mind switched back to Lorraine. What could have
happened to her? He started thinking, trying to remember how old
he was when he first met Lorraine. The exact year eluded him but
some of the incidents from those school years were permanently

etched in his mind. As he lay in bed, he envisioned himself in grade five. Lorraine and this fellow... Lincoln Alexander Hoffmann, had enrolled in his class. The kids called Lincoln 'El Sicko' or 'Sick' for short, or politely just 'Alex' when they wanted to be nice because they were asking for a favour. The latter wasn't very often.

Hoffmann's father was a German Jew who had immigrated to Canada sometime in the seventies. The old man owned a jewelry store downtown. McCall remembered one time when he was handing him back his repaired watch, he noticed some tattooed numbers on his forearm. McCall had no idea what those numbers meant. He recalled thinking perhaps they represented some Jewish identification number or his tag number during the war.

Hoffmann always had money. His father was a horologist, making and repairing timepieces. Sicko used to tell some incredible stories about his father during the war including when he was enlisted and then later when he was placed in a concentration camp. His father had been forced to engrave countless gold items confiscated from wealthy Jews. He had been ordered to remove the original owner's name from trophies and gold jewellery and replace the engravings with a fictitious name. He also engraved some Iron Crosses and numerous gold medals.

None of the school kids ever saw El Sicko's mother and they wondered if he even had one. In their opinion he had been hatched. He wore round wire-rimmed glasses that made him look bug-eyed. He was skinny and certainly not very strong. However he didn't need to be strong because no one had ever challenged him to a fight. The girls, mainly Lorraine, were the ones who spoke to him most of the time and they probably did that out of pity. He used to call Lorraine 'mommy' and the girls called him Alex. He was very smart, though and always had good grades. Alex was the only person the kids had ever known who gave them the creeps with his mere appearance. He had dirty brown hair and it didn't matter whether he had it long or short, it always looked a mess. And he had terrible acne all over his face.

McCall reminisced about the time when they were in grade five. It was a sunny summer day. He had just finished his lunch out in the schoolyard. He decided to go into the classroom to retrieve some money from his well hidden stash. As he entered the classroom he saw a group of kids huddled near an open window.

He heard Lorraine cry out, "Oh, no - gross, freak me out, yuck".

McCall couldn't imagine what was going on so he went closer to the window and saw Hoffmann sitting on the window sill. He was holding a magnifying glass and directing the sun onto his bare left forearm until the skin puffed up into a blister and started to smoke. He already had five or six burn marks on his arm. Thank God for the open window because the smell of burning human flesh almost made him puke. In spite of all that, Lorraine, for some ungodly reason, touched his arm as if she felt sorry for him.

The abduction started flooding McCall's mind again. He felt so totally helpless. How could he do anything when he didn't know anything. He had to get some sleep because holy hell would undoubtedly break out tomorrow. As a matter of fact it was tomorrow already, half past one, early Saturday morning.

This Hoffmann fellow kept creeping back into his thoughts. This time Alex was bragging to some guys that he could hit his arm with the edge of a ruler so hard that his skin would puff up into welts. McCall got a clear vision of Hoffmann hitting his arm with a ruler with the skin puffing up wherever he hit. And there was Lorraine again, touching the humps on his arm and asking him if it hurt. El Sicko replied it didn't. Of course there were always some who had to try the same thing, and naturally, got the same results. The next day there were a dozen guys with black horizontal bruise marks all over their arms.

He really had to get some sleep he kept telling himself. Lorraine will probably call him in the morning. Something must have come up. She will call. Who knows? As loans manager the bank might have required her to travel on a moment's notice. And who knows, she could have called him when he wasn't available. Maybe she had called and someone had forgotten to give him the message. She could have become involved in the investigation she had talked about the other day. She could have flown to the head office in B.C. to work on the case of the former crooked manager of loans who had embezzled money by writing up loans to non-existent people. Until now he hadn't realized how much Lorraine meant to him. He missed her pretty tanned face, her velvety brown hair, her sparkling green eyes, her tender touch, her witty mind and her cheerful laughter. To him she was the most attractive woman ever - even with her clothes on.
It was interesting that they hadn't seen each other since their high school graduation. Then, one evening about five years ago, they ran into each other at the Toronto International Airport and immediately hit it off.

No matter what he did, he couldn't fall asleep or get Lorraine or the abduction out of his mind. It was now 2:53 am. That bus came back to haunt his thoughts again. He had to get rid of that. He remembered that warm milk was supposed to help people get to sleep. He got up and went through his cupboards. After some searching he found some milk powder. Using some hot water from the tap he made something white that resembled milk and drank it. It tasted like plaster and it didn't work. Not for him, anyway. He lay down again and fantasized about being the deputy chief or maybe even the chief. There was a good possibility Chief Stewart might retire soon. Especially after this mess. He couldn't recall any abductions since he'd been with the force. Usually when there was one, demands were made right away. And usually for a great amount of money. To have 'thirty' passengers disappear into thin air was simply absurd. He figured

CBC and CNN would have a blast with this bizarre situation. The Canadian Air Force would be put on red alert along with the US Air Force. No question about it, this had the makings of something big.

Enough of this bull, he started telling himself. He began counting sheep, then plain numbers. No sleep came. He forced himself to think of his school years again. Hoffmann resurfaced in his mind. He was back in the school again. In those days they still had corporal punishment but only the incorrigible had to fear it. He wasn't one of them. Hoffmann was.

One day the class went wild. Every time their music teacher turned his back to write something on the blackboard, Hoffmann reflected the sunlight onto his bald head using his pocket mirror. Whenever he did that the whole class broke into crazy laughter. One time he got bold and followed the beam down the teacher's arm. When the teacher saw the reflection on the blackboard, he swung around quickly and caught Hoffmann with the mirror in his hand. Usually that particular teacher was a mild tempered, good humoured man. However this time, his face including his bald head, turned crimson red and like a raging bull he lunged at Hoffmann. With shaking hands he snatched the mirror and within a few seconds it became history as it hit the floor and shattered into a million pieces. He asked Hoffmann for his hand. Hoffmann knew exactly what was coming. Since he was right handed he stuck out his left palm. The teacher raised his stick, and when it was about to make contact, Hoffmann jerked it back and the twenty-four inch stick crashed onto the desk and became a four inch stick. At this point the teacher's face and high forehead turned snow white. All the kids in the classroom fell dead silent. As he stared at the four inch stick, Hoffmann's life flashed before his eyes. The teacher reached into his pocket and pulled out a jack knife. He opened it and with a tremulous voice he said to Hoffmann,

"Do you see that bush out there in the yard?" and he pointed to the open window.

Hoffmann didn't have to look. Everybody knew where the bush was. There was only one bush.

Hoffmann answered, "Yes sir."

Then the teacher said, "I want you to go out there with this jack knife" and he handed Hoffmann the handsome piece of cutlery "and I want you to cut me another stick just like the one I had, and bring it back. Understand, Hoffmann!"

"Yes sir," he answered again.

Hoffmann took the knife and regarded it like a lizard might regard a cobra. He sullenly walked to the door. He turned around to take a last look at the class because for sure the teacher would kill him when he returned. McCall remembered Hoffmann as a thinker. He figured out if he didn't have a knife he couldn't cut a stick. And if there was no stick, he couldn't be beaten to death. He stuck the knife into a sturdy cleft and pushed on it. Bingo, the blade broke. With a doleful look on his face, he sauntered back into the classroom holding the now two piece jack knife in his hand. He walked to the teacher's desk and told him the knife had broken. Again there was dead silence in the room. The teacher's pallid high forehead and face turned crimson red once more. Then, as if a bomb exploded, the buzzer sounded. Hoffmann was saved by the bell.

McCall got up and turned on the lights. It was 3:06. Where are you Lorraine? Please call me he cried out loud at her picture on his dresser. The picture didn't answer. So he didn't ask again. He went to the cupboard and took out a bottle of whiskey and had a good swig. He emptied his bladder and turned on CBC. It was all about WRL and the 'thirty' abducted passengers. He switched to CNN. Everyone was talking about the abduction and assuming great amounts of ransom would be demanded. Still, there was no ransom demand from anyone. This was the most unusual abduction ever, everyone said. The whisky was starting to make him drowsy so he went back to bed. But sleep still didn't come. He must have rolled over a dozen times, and couldn't fall asleep. He had to get some sleep. He must get some sleep. It'll be hell on earth in the morning.

He started reminiscing some more but figured at this rate he'd soon be out of things to reminisce about. This time he was in grade eight and his home room teacher was a Mr. Armstrong. Armstrong told his students that if no one failed, he would take them up north to his cottage for a weekend. His cottage was at Eagle Hills which was an extension of Blue Mountain. In the winter it was a popular place for skiers. In the summertime it was known for its lakes of crystal clear water and sandy beaches. They all studied like crazy and everyone passed.

As promised, early one summer morning with tents, blankets, sleeping bags and coolers full of pop (with the odd bottle of booze on the bottom) the kids boarded a chartered bus and rolled out of the schoolyard. For the next two blocks, pyjama-clad parents waved goodbye through open car windows.
As they rumbled down the street, McCall remembered the smell of sweet diesel smoke, even inside the bus. He was already addicted to diesel fumes. Their bus driver was a well dressed young man in his late twenties. His grey uniform included a military style hat that perfectly complemented his curly light brown hair. His black tie and white shirt accentuated his tanned Roman face. Eleven drooling girls sat behind Armstrong who sat protectively directly behind the driver. The guys were settled at the back of the bus with the exception of three or four diehards near the girls. Hoffmann and a guy named Dave Mannen being two of them. Hoffmann, as usual, was trying to show off to the girls with his macho man impersonations.
None of the girls paid any attention to him except Lorraine. She thought he was funny. McCall had found out later that she had actually had a crush on him and would have dated him had he asked. It wasn't that he didn't like her, he just wasn't interested in

girls at that time. In those days Lorraine was a mother image to him and everybody. She was the type of girl who already looked nubile at the age of thirteen. She was also one of the top students in the class and always participated in everything. He could still picture her with her 40D bust chasing after a basketball. He always thought the running would hurt her. McCall looked at the clock again and rubbed his eyes. It was 3:15. Then, just like in the movies, the school bus appeared again in his mind and he was once more at the back of the bus. This was the nerve centre, the planning room. There they were, full of ideas and laughing it up like crazy. Once in a while a girl would go back to see them as a goodwill ambassador, but after a few minutes of conversation she'd leave with burning ears.

As McCall recollected the trip to the cottage, took about two hours and it was two hours of steady foolishness and laughter until their jaws ached. To top it all off, along came Hoffmann with his thumbs bent back touching his wrists and the tip of his tongue in one of his nostrils. He was trying to imitate a maniac. He didn't seem to impress Lorraine that time, but he broke everybody else up.

Dreamily McCall remembered just after that display, the bus slowed and made a right turn. Next he heard gravel bouncing against the bus undercarriage. As he looked through the tinted window a sense of elation came over him. Then he saw some tall pine trees behind flat leafed water lilies. There was a marsh on either side of the road. They got to higher ground and slowed down again. They made a right turn again and this time their own dust caught up to them. The bus stopped and the robot arm opened the exit door. Armstrong got out and unlocked the chain on the property entrance gate and jumped back onto the bus. He motioned to the driver to go through. Two or three hundred yards further there was a clearing and beyond that to the right there was a small lake. Straight ahead a few yards there was a weather-beaten log cabin. McCall remembered thinking it was the coolest cabin he'd ever seen.

With excitement creating total pandemonium everyone got off the bus. McCall took one more long sniff of the diesel fumes then joined his friends. They congratulated each other with their usual palm slap and cheered Armstrong. The teacher announced that until Sunday at 6 pm they were on their own. But before he let them go, they had to listen to the rules and formalities. He advised everyone that Lake Huron was about a mile away and if they wanted to go there they would have to let him know who was going and when they were coming back. McCall sensed Armstrong would have preferred they stayed put and went swimming in his little lake. There were even fish in the lake, Armstrong said, but he knew none of the kids had come here to go fishing.

He also told them the rules of the outhouse. He wanted the guys to use it for number two only. He didn't want them peeing on the wooden toilet seat. He said the kerosene lamp was left burning in the john all night for convenience. He asked the guys not to loiter around the outhouse and to knock before entering. For any questions they were to see him. The rules were commonsense rules. Fires were permitted in designated areas only. Armstrong said he had scheduled a bonfire for Saturday evening down at the clearing by his lake. The first aid kit was in the cabin on the wall next to the door. He showed them the water push pump and how to use it. The water was a little sulphuric but potable. He told everybody that his property consisted of ten acres and the fence around the cabin was there to protect the fruit trees from the deer. The barbed wire on top was to keep unwanted hunters out. There was a gate behind the cabin that he would keep open for their convenience. They weren't supposed to wander too far because of the possibility of bears or wild boars. McCall remembered Armstrong went on for a few more minutes that seemed like hours. Finally he dismissed them and they scattered like mercury from a broken thermometer.

The minute they left Armstrong they divided into groups,

and situated themselves in different areas. McCall and a couple of guys put their tents up a good distance away from the girls, while Hoffmann and Mannen put their tents up a short distance from them. They unpacked their stuff and listened to music that was loud enough to wake the dead. They spent most of the day exploring their immediate area, went swimming and played soccer. It was a super day.

It was early evening, he remembered and they were almost ready to quit the soccer game when they heard an awful shrill scream coming from the little lake area. They stopped dead in their tracks. McCall remembered thinking someone must have jumped into the water and gotten hurt. They all started running towards that desperate scream. Lorraine motioned to him and wanted to say something but couldn't get it out. Finally she managed a, "There... there... by the deck. There's a dead body in the water."

He was the first one down the bank and shuddered as he laid eyes upon the corpse. It was a male body submerged about six inches below the water. He was face up. There was seaweed around his mouth and his torso, but his eyeballs... they appeared flipped out of their sockets. He shuddered again. He tried to reach down to grab a hold of the body to pull it out, but changed his mind because he remembered that sometimes a limb might fall off depending on how long the body had been in the water.

By this time everyone was on the bank and waiting for his next move. Thinking back, perhaps he should have gone to get Armstrong but at the time it didn't occur to him. The sight of those Monty Python eyes staring at him from a grotesque green face had him momentarily hypnotized. He couldn't recall what prompted him, but he got an uncontrollable urge to stir the body. He bent down to pick up a sturdy looking branch and at that same moment a gulp of air froze in his throat. He watched as a murky green face rose from the water. A thin ray of the setting sun reflected on the whites of those rolled back eyes as the pupils

41

made a complete circle and finally centred in their sockets.
He staggered. He remembered feeling as though he was holding a
shorted-out electrical circuit. His brain signalled his legs to
straighten up but instead his leg muscles relaxed. His brain
signalled his neck muscles to turn his head and his neck turned
but his eyes remained focused. His brain signalled his feet to run
but instead they stayed immobile. His brain signalled his vocal
chords to scream but his voice remained mute. He heard blood
curdling cries behind him and thuds on the ground. He realized
some people had fainted. Something had to be done. He grabbed
the stick in his hand and raised it to above his head. McCall
remembered he was about to strike the creature, who had by now,
completely emerged from the water and was spitting seaweed and
a plastic hose from its mouth and yelling at him to stop.

It was Hoffmann.

All McCall could utter was, "Hoffmann, you son of a
bitch".
That day is engraved in his mind for ever.
Now he was starting to feel tired and exhausted. He settled
on counting green zombies and finally fell asleep.

CHAPTER 3

To get away from constant interruptions that Friday afternoon, Lorraine had gone home at 3pm to finish her report in peace. She made duplicates of her work and put one copy in an envelope for the bank. She put a red dot in the corner of the original for easy identification. She then put all the papers in her briefcase and packed her luggage with clothes enough for a six month vacation. She placed the luggage by the kitchen door. She turned off the air conditioning and made sure everything else was off. She watered the plants, picked up her keys and luggage and entered the hallway. The kitchen door locked automatically behind her. She walked to the building exit a little way down the hall.

Through the glass exit door, a paperboy saw her coming. He quickly entered in front of her with his papers and flyers and started stuffing them into her mailbox.

"Oh I'll take those," Lorraine said. The boy took the newspaper out of the mailbox and purposely dropped a yellow flyer. The sheet of paper floated to the floor and landed blank side up. He fumbled around with the stack of yellow sheets and purposely dropped all of them
The WRL rail advertisement flyers were all over the floor. Some

43

face up, some face down.

     "Oh, don't worry about the advertising, I never read it anyway," Lorraine said to the paperboy chuckling. But her subconscious mind had read it already. As he gathered up the leaflets, he stuck one into Lorraine's paper anyway and gave it to her and headed towards the next building. Half way there, he stopped and placed all the papers onto the concrete walkway to straighten them out. In a clandestine manner he was watching Lorraine's every move. When she got to her car she pushed the remote trunk button but nothing happened. She pushed the button a few more times with no results. She wondered how this could have happened. She could have sworn that she locked the car when she came home because she did that instinctively. She got into the car and found the interior trunk button didn't work either. She placed the newspaper on the passenger seat and turned on the ignition. The car didn't start. She turned the key again. Nothing. She hesitated for a moment and pushed the dome light switch. No lights. She tried the radio, the radio was dead too. She searched for the hood latch. She popped the hood and got out of the car. To her greatest surprise the battery was gone. The connecting wires were dangling in the air. Great, she said to herself... vandalism... I'll have to see if they took anything else from inside the car and started looking in the glove compartment and the door pockets. Nothing else was missing.

     What now... how was she going to get to Toronto. She thought about McCall coming to pick her up but then remembered he was at work. Now what, she said to herself again.

     She thought of calling her dealership for a loaner. Then she thought she might call her insurance company about renting a car. Suddenly she remembered the yellow flyer from the WRL train advertising. There it was right in front of her. She would call and find out when the next train to Toronto was. Great idea, she praised herself. Rather than spend time memorizing her notes at McCall's place, she could do that on the train.

     She took the key out of the ignition, gathered up the newspaper and yellow pamphlet and luggage in hand she returned to her apartment. Upon seeing her re-enter the building, the paperboy punched a set of numbers into a cell phone and got a connection on the first ring.

"She's gone back to her apartment," the paperboy said into the cell phone.

"Great, I'll take it from here. Hey... thanks. I guess you're all done. You did a fine job, you'll get the rest of your five hundred bucks in the mail next week. See ya."

~

Sitting in a tour bus in view of the railroad tracks, but well off Highway 403, Charles Parker, aka Lincoln Alexander Hoffman got the good news from his accomplice - the paperboy. Using a linesman phone he punched in Lorraine's phone number.

He heard Lorraine dialing the WRL ticket office in St. Thomas. A clerk answered and said there was lots of room on the train and there was plenty of time before departure.

"Excellent," she rejoiced.

She looked up her dealership's number and phoned the service department. The service manager said he'd come to pick her up and take her to the train station in time to catch the six o'clock train and they'd have the car fixed on Monday. She replied that there was no need to hurry because she wouldn't be back from her vacation for three weeks.

"Well, we'll have it done anyway," the service manager said.

~

As six pm approached Parker dialled his technician crew who were waiting in a pickup truck close to Two Mile Bridge and gave them his order,

"Cut the tab at six fifteen."

An eager technician answered, "No problem."

Excitement rippled through Parker's body and he felt like he was thirteen again. He was a mischievous kid again. His elaborate plan was starting to take shape. Finally, he would be close to Lorraine, his 'mommy' again... even if just for an hour, or a day. To be near her is worth everything. After years of craving motherly love, craving for a scolding when he did something wrong, he'd have his mommy. He'd feel her soft touch on his arm. He had worked out the details and things were falling into place just fine... but now he had to concentrate on the time.

If the train was going at 100 km per hour, it would reach Brantford in thirty minutes. He counted the seats and decided he'd pick up thirty people. He summarised his final details once more and checked the tires. Everything was meticulously ready.

Feeling very pleased with himself, Parker got back onto the bus, inhaled deeply and started the engine. Shifting into first gear, then into second, he drove out to the paved road and onto Highway 403 that headed towards Brantford.

~

With her bulky suitcase in hand, Lorraine made her way down the coach aisle looking for an empty compartment. About midway she found one and went inside. She made herself comfortable and got her report out of her briefcase. Just as she began reading, a well dressed middle aged man cracked open the door and asked if he could come in.

There goes my reading she thought, and with a muffled sigh she said, "Come on in."

"I can go and look for another place," the man said meekly.

"No, no, just come on in. I don't own this cabin," Lorraine said.

"My name is George Date. Sorry to interrupt you. Maybe I should go to another compartment," Date said with a grin as he stuck out his hand for a handshake none the less.

Lorraine found Date pleasant and polite and assured him it was alright. She shook his hand as she introduced herself and moved closer to the window.

Date appeared a little embarrassed about disturbing her and apologized profusely.

"No problem, Mr. Date, I was just going to review some of my reports," she said as she slid the papers back in her briefcase.

Date put his bag on the rack above the seats and sized up her bulky suitcase and asked if she wanted it on the rack too.

"Oh probably, just in case someone else might want to come in. It's not heavy," she laughed, "It's just full of clothes."

Date picked up the suitcase and swung it onto the rack, and sat down opposite Lorraine.

"You know... ah... I don't imagine you're interested, but I've been going crazy thinking about my son and my daughter in-law." Date said while making himself comfortable on his seat. Clearing his throat he continued, "My son George Jr. is a musician and says he's going to be a rock star someday. Yeah... like I'll be the Prime Minister. He travels all over the country with his band, and sends his wife Denise money but it's not enough for her to live on. She has a job as a secretary in a lawyer's office and has a little girl, and that's another thing... My son insisted on naming her Ecstasy. Can you imagine what life is going to be like for a girl called Ecstasy Date? Especially in school." Lorraine was actually amused. Stifling a giggle, she looked out the window and thought of Johnny Cash and his song 'The Boy Named Sue'. She wound up saying, "Oh my God, mister Date." Luckily, Date said something funny about his son's spiked green hair and she burst out laughing. Date continued, "Denise has a heck of a time finding a babysitter. I have a little money but I'm retired now. I didn't want to retire, but my company bit the dust and everybody was let go. My wife left me years ago because we were always fighting about the kids. She wanted to let them do their own thing and I didn't. I have another son, his name is Roger... He's thirty one. Two years younger than George Jr. Rodger went to university and learned Chinese. Now he's in China, teaching English to Chinese kids. At least he has a good job.

Date talked a mile a minute. He was a charming person and his voice was pleasant. He sounded sincere, Lorraine thought and she just let him carry on.

As the train clattered along, blowing its whistle occasionally, a crackling sound came from the speaker and an announcement was made. The announcer said that there was a train derailment at Two Mile Bridge. The train was going to stop in Brantford and the passengers were going to be taken by bus to Union Station in Toronto.

Lorraine was surprised. What the heck...what else could go wrong, she said aloud and began to explain, "I had to take the train because someone stole the battery from my car, and now I have to take a bus. Next I'll probably have to take a boat or an air plane. Isn't that funny Mr. Date?"

"You don't say. Where was your car?"

"Right in my parking spot at my apartment. I've been living there for five years and nothing like this ever happened before. It's a good place to live. My neighbours are ghosts. I never see them. The rent is reasonable and all I have to pay is the phone and the internet. And they are on PAP."

"Guess somebody needed a battery more than you did," Date said with a sympathetic look.

"I guess," she said, and looked out the window absentmindedly. The train started to slow down.

"This must be Brantford," Date said as he got Lorraine's bulky suitcase off the rack. "I'll help you with that," he said and the two of them left the compartment. Lorraine thanked him and followed him down the aisle.

In Brantford the conductor came around checking for sleeping passengers and made sure everyone had heard the announcement.

As the two got off the train, a light rain drizzled and Lorraine hurried to get inside the train station. The double doors of the waiting room had been opened and inside the air smelled of mothballs and aromatic pipe tobacco. One man said if cigarettes smelled that nice, he wouldn't have quit smoking. Everyone let that go without any comment. Some people stayed outside and lit up cigarettes.

The man who had been smoking the pipe introduced himself to the passengers as Ed Clement, the former stationmaster. He told them he had retired from his regular job when the station was decommissioned but stayed on as caretaker.

To pass the time, Clement started showing the passengers some interesting old posters on the walls. While he was doing this, a bus arrived and began picking up some of the passengers.

After having looked at only a few of the posters, Lorraine and Date were picked right off the bat. The bus filled up quickly and was on its way immediately.

Lorraine sat down by the window on the left hand side of the bus and Date sat opposite her. When the bus reached the highway, the driver introduced himself as Charles Parker. He said he was an experienced driver and had driven all over North America. He said the best highways were in Canada. Some trips were long and lonely though, like those to British Columbia. But he had always made the travellers time fly, by telling interesting stories of places few had ever seen. The passengers were mesmerized.

"We have such a place not far from Toronto. Has anyone ever heard of Eagle Hills Resort?" This question was a loaded one to see if Lorraine remembered. No one answered, although a tiny bell did ring in Lorraine's mind.

She thought she had heard of that place before but couldn't remember for sure. Parker continued, "A few years ago a numbered company purchased the land around Eagle Hills. A

49

couple of years construction began on a resort complex. Over one hundred vacation units have already been built. There is an Olympic-sized swimming pool; a bowling alley; pool tables; volleyball and tennis courts as well as a racquetball court. There is a brand new casino. Plans are underway for a theme park including a roller-coaster. There will even be facilities for holding boat races on the local lake."

Lorraine was still thinking about that name Eagle Hills. Parker's mellow voice carried on but no one had the foggiest idea what he was getting at.

He continued, "There will be ski runs with lifts in the nearby mountains. There will be saunas and hot tubs at the ski resort area. There will be restaurants, bars, grocery stores and a hospital. There will be a state of the art security system with a network of cameras and there will be a bank." For greater effect Parker purposely mentioned the bank last. Then he said,

"This type of entertainment resort is not a new idea but it is new for Canada. There are resorts like this in the United States and now there is going to be one in Ontario."
He went on with details and descriptions of many other exciting amenities.

Date was sitting opposite Lorraine with his mouth open in total amazement. He didn't know there was a development like this in Ontario. He asked Lorraine if she had ever heard of this place. She shook her head but in her thoughts was the name Eagle Hills. That name! That name, she thought. Why does that sound so familiar? She still couldn't connect the name to any place she knew of.

By now, it was getting dark. The city lights had disappeared. No one noticed that the bus had left the main highway and was driving down a country road. Everybody was still hanging on Parker's words.

When he started talking about the Arab Emirates where people didn't have to work at all, some of the passengers gasped.

"Their wealth came from natural resources, like oil and

gas under the sand. Wouldn't it be nice if Canada had the same resources? It could be that way in Canada too. We have the 'oil sands' in Alberta. Just imagine, if people didn't have to work here either... We wouldn't even have to pay income tax". Everyone laughed.

The bus arrived at a crossroad and as it turned right, some gravel bounced off the undercarriage. It pulled off to the side of the road and stopped.

Facing the passengers now and clearing his throat, Parker began, "Ladies and gentlemen, I have something really exciting and amazing to tell you. Is everybody sitting down?"Everyone was bewildered and silent.

"Ladies and gentlemen, this is a million dollar extraordinary marketing event. Such an undertaking has never been tried in Canada before. I have been authorized to give each and every one of you twenty-five thousand Canadian dollars. I repeat, everyone is getting twenty-five thousand dollars for keeping this event a secret for two days. Two days only! You will be given five shares in the resort business, which will be worth a lot of money down the road. On top of all that, you will also receive one thousand dollars to play in our casino, and if you win you can keep your winnings. There's more. You'll stay in your private room at this Eagle Hills Resort for two days and two nights. Tonight and tomorrow you will be treated like royalty and pampered in luxury. We will cater to your every personal need and want. You don't have to worry about any change of clothes, because if you need anything you can get it for free from the resort 'STORES'. The meals are made by our chefs. Drinks of any kind... Everything is on the house. There is still more. If you wish to work for us we are hiring now, you will get a chance to apply for a position at the resort. If you're not qualified for the job you chose, we will send you to school at company expense. We are looking for honest and loyal employees in all trades. The goal of this resort is to show the world that there is still a right way of doing business. Too often the ordinary people, the workers are forgotten. To most businesses, money is the only thing that matters. Now, ladies and gentlemen, there is a slight caveat... and I am sure everyone has been waiting for this. Since we want to shock the world with our event, we have only one request of you, during your stay with us and it starts now. You cannot use your wireless devices to text or make a phone call to anyone. This bold and stunning event will fail and will have to be abandoned if outside people get wind of it. It is imperative that everything stays secret... until you get home. Once this extraordinary two day event is completed, you can call anybody or do whatever you want. You will be twenty-five thousand dollars richer and set for life. You may become famous. You will be popular, if you want to be... believe me. There will be media people asking you about your lucky adventure and your good fortune. We want to show the world there is still room for innovative thinking, compassion, happiness and kindness. We want to build our reputation on trust. We will require perfection from our associates, vendors and contractors and we will offer total satisfaction to our clientele and patrons. We want to show the world that there is still a way to make an honest dollar. Our investors will share their wealth with the people, which is in itself magnanimous, and I emphasize this has never been done before."

Everyone on the bus was silent and shocked.

Parker continued, "This looks like a kidnapping on the surface, and that is exactly what we want it to look like, we want worldwide exposure. We want all the media to scream about this, sensationalize this. We want all the newspapers, tabloids, televisions and radios blaring, calling us criminals and villains. This event is intended to change how rich people of the world think. We want to show the upper class, the millionaires how to put their wealth to good use. But you know this is not a real abduction because you are free to go. However if you decide to leave, you will forfeit all the money and will only get a ride to your destination. We are at a crossroad now, where you decide to either stay or go. I have taxis waiting down the road." Parker pointed to a row of taxi tail lights visible a short distance away.

"I'll give you some time to think this over and to make up your mind. Please think about all that money and what you can do with it. We are at the resort now. If you stay the money will be transferred to your bank account immediately or you will be given a certified cheque for the twenty-five thousand dollars. The wireless communication has been disabled".

Like everyone else, Lorraine was flabbergasted. Aside from the money, she might get a chance to be a bank manager at this resort. As for Date, it would give him an opportunity to re-enter the work force, which he hadn't wanted to leave in the first place.

"What do you think of this?" Date asked Lorraine as he scrutinized the faces of the people.

"I am stunned," she said. "This is fabulous."

The bus was abuzz with excited conversation. Most of the people were dazzled by the amount of money.

"I'm going to see what the others are thinking," Date said to Lorraine as he got up from his seat and started talking with some of the passengers. Not surprisingly, everyone was on board with the offer. "Please raise your hand if you have decided to stay," Parker said. Everyone raised their hand immediately so Parker flicked his headlights at the taxis. The taxi drivers signalled back.

"Thank you very much," Parker said and continued "we are moments away from the resort office." Everyone clapped.

Lorraine thought this was a good deal, and she was going to take advantage of it. The bank at Eagle Hills had her hooked.

As Date sat down Parker shifted into drive. The bus was going uphill now and passing a marsh on either side of the road. Then it took a right turn. A little ways ahead through a row of pine trees, the bright lights of a large resort became visible.

Date turned to Lorraine and said, "Ms. Wilkinson, I wouldn't have believed it, but I think we have just arrived in Shangri-la."

As for Parker's plan, had there been any dissension, another five thousand dollars would have been added to the offer. Money meant nothing to Parker.

CHAPTER 4

The bus pulled up to the resort security gate. An attendant opened the gate and stepped back into the guardhouse. As he drove through, Parker waved to man. After driving a short distance the bus stopped in front of a large building and Parker got out. Standing aside, he shook hands with all the passengers as they got off the bus.

"Welcome to Eagle Hills" he said, holding Lorraine's hand just a tad longer.

Even though Lorraine's touch lasted only a moment, it was long enough to awaken a feeling in him. A feeling he had tucked away for almost twenty years. That warm tingling feeling cascaded into every cell in his body. The idle tension that had built up inside him over the years was finally gone. With blood rushing to his head and with his vision blurring, he steadied himself on the side of the bus. This time the feeling was a lot stronger and quite different from the good old days. This feeling was comparable to an earthquake. An earthquake that shook his entire body. It was a climax that cascaded from somewhere in his head and trickled down all the way to his toes. This kind of feeling he'd never experienced before and this time he didn't understand it.

Had she been observing him, she would have noticed a slight tremor on his face, but she didn't look at Parker because she was watching her step.

~

At the entrance of the three-storey building were two young women in white blouses and grey skirts warmly welcoming everyone. Facing the front door and at the far end of the lavishly decorated hall were the registration counters. However since this was a special occasion, the registration was taking place at a table on the right hand side of the hall. Susan Crandall, one of the young women, came and sat down behind a table with a laptop and a box of blank name tags.

To the left of Ms. Crandall were several tables with hors d'oeuvres.

Once everyone was inside, another young woman, Barbara House with a very pleasing voice informed the passengers that dinner would be served shortly in the great dining hall behind Ms. Crandall's table. Beverages were available from circulating waiters. Ms. Crandall asked the passengers to come and get their gifts – the twenty-five thousand dollars and their gaming chips and their name tags.

A piano played in the dining room and the sound of a lovely melody filtered through the open dining room doors. Sweet fragrance of exotic flowers floated in the air. There were beautiful patterned sofas and easy chairs throughout the entire hall.

Smartly dressed waiters glided amongst the now relaxed and happy passengers and through a hallway domed windows could be seen decorated with expensive oriental drapes. The registration proceeded quickly and the $25,000 deposit was indeed reality.

As Ms. Crandall recorded the passengers, she pinned on their name tags and asked them to take a seat and relax until they were all registered.

Everyone's profession and vocation was being openly

documented except for two table dancers who pretended to be beautician students from Toronto. They didn't want to disclose their occupation. This of course made no difference to Ms. Crandall.

The waiters were busy with bar orders and had been prepared to answer a most questions asked. Parker had gone to his room to change into a pair of light coloured cotton pants and a yellow polo shirt. He joined Lorraine who was wearing tight fitting shorts with a patterned t-shirt. She was sitting with Date on a large sofa behind an enormous coffee table. Upon seeing Parker, a waiter went to serve him immediately. Lorraine and Date had already asked for and gotten their drinks. She ordered a Black Russian and Date had a gin and tonic. Parker ordered vodka on ice.

"May I sit with you?" Parker asked Lorraine with a somewhat uncertain smile.

"We would be honoured Mr. Parker," Lorraine said.

There was something strange about this man. She had met him before, but where... she couldn't place him. Even his voice seemed familiar.

"So, Ms. Wilkinson, how are you doing so far?"

"Fabulous, everything is beautiful. I think you're on the right track, Mr. Parker," Lorraine said as she shook Parker's outreached hand again, this time warmly. Parker's hand burned from her touch.

"And how do you do, Mr. Date,"

"Oh, I'm on top of the world," Date said and went on ranting and raving about the beauty of the place and how he met Lorraine on the train. All the while Parker was swimming in a sea of delight, he was in seventh heaven. Shaking Lorraine's hand again had brought back feelings that he could have died for.

Parker sat down on an easy chair opposite Lorraine and Date and started talking banking business. Being too technical a conversation for Date, he excused himself and went to check out some more of the amenities. After Date left, Parker continued with his vision of the new bank at the resort. He watched

Lorraine's reaction and was happy to see elation and genuine concern on her face. He could see she knew what he was talking about.

Without getting into too much detail, Lorraine told Parker she was currently investigating a fraudulent case for her bank. Parker didn't press her; he was just overjoyed that their reunion had gone so well. Once in a while her expression stiffened and her eyes narrowed. However the reason for this could have been her pondering over her investigation or perhaps she was thinking about her boyfriend. But for Parker, nothing else except his personal needs mattered. And those needs were numerous.

Coddling a drink, Date returned voicing praises about the facilities and complimenting Parker on his good taste. Parker accepted the compliments gracefully. Not that he wouldn't want to stay with Lorraine all the time. Parker wanted to savour the time with her and decided to slow down. One step at a time! He apologized to Lorraine and Date and said he wanted to meet some of the other passengers before dinner started. While leaving, he asked the two if he could join them later at their table. Lorraine said they would be delighted.

~

There were several small groups in the hall, and their animated conversation gave Parker the assurance he was doing things the right way. He'd circulated among them cheerfully and when it was time for dinner, everyone entered the large dining room. With the help of two waiters, all the passengers were settled at their choice of tables.

The solid oak dining room tables were covered with white tablecloths and sparkling silverware. The soft backed chairs were covered in the same luxurious patterned fabric as the sofas and easy chairs in the hall. The wall coverings were a diffused red with walnut wainscoting. Elaborate chandeliers adorned the ceiling and the flickering light from candle shaped sconces illuminated the walls and the curtains of the stage.

There were original paintings by Lenny Horne, Vic Gibbons, Robert Bateman Jim Jackson, Sandra Stewart, Sally Robert, Margaret Brock and Lynn Kennedy and others. Scattered throughout the rooms were important fine paintings from Hungary that spoke volumes about the classiness of this fine establishment.

The seating of thirty passengers used up only a small portion of the large dining room which was designed to hold two hundred people.

The piano player who had been on the stage, entertaining the passengers, took a bow and turned the stage over to Parker. Parker began to announce his plans for the night.

"After dinner once you have settled in your rooms, you are free to do whatever you wish. You can gamble or go swimming. Bathing suits and other garments are available from the STORES. There is an old fashion ' jukebox' and a dance floor in the bar. All the other facilities are also open. Since you are the only guests, you have the entire resort and personnel at your service. For our advertising purposes and publicity, there will be photographers taking pictures throughout the weekend. There are makeup artists and hair stylists for those who wish to use these services. Since we would like genuine reaction on your faces, please act naturally when you are being photographed. You are all important movie stars this weekend.

From time to time there will be an announcements made regarding various activities, games or prizes. Don't be startled if one of our staff addresses you by name as they are practising total recall. They only have to remember thirty names now but they'll have a tougher time with hundreds of guests.

All rooms are private! If you feel that your privacy is tampered with, or invaded in any way, which is of course highly unlikely, get in touch with me. I can be reached through any of the house phones. You don't have to worry about making an outside call by accident as the regular phones are not connected to the public lines. And of course, as you are aware, cell phone services have been disabled on the resort property.

Every room is furnished with a mini bar that you are welcome to use. They do not require a key, however... and I ask you please... do not over indulge. I don't want you to miss out on all the fun. Just one more thing, our goal is to attract people from all over the world. This company believes the best way to discover people is through their various cultural foods. Since one of our principle share holders is from Hungary, we are honouring him on this special day, with Hungarian cuisine. We are proud of the fact that Hungarian cuisine is known and appreciated throughout the world. Our chefs are the best of Hungary and they will demonstrate their skills to you tonight. They will be introduced after dinner. For now I will ask the head chef to tell you the secret of Hungarian culinary art. Ladies and gentlemen, please welcome master chef Matthew Harai."

Stepping out from behind some curtains and saying hello, in a typical Hungarian accent the master chef began, "In Hungary, it is not just the preparing of tasteful dishes that is important, but also how they are served; one after the other, always whetting the appetite for the next one is important. And when you think you have had just enough, another course is served that makes you say: I must try this too. But I am sure you will decide that all by yourselves." Harai clapped his hand, twice.

As the chef left the stage, Parker said: "Jo etvagyat." But the pronunciation was horrible and one of the passengers, a young Hungarian man cut in and said the two words in proper Hungarian. Parker thanked him for that.

"Anyway the words mean Bon Appetit, or good appetite. Enjoy your evening everyone." Hooting and hollering and applause followed as Parker sat down at Lorraine's table.

Parker's staff occupied a fair part of the dining room near the kitchen. One of his managers, Dallas Matheson waved him over. He apologized to Lorraine and Date and promised to return momentarily.

Dinner consisted of five courses: the first course was chicken dumpling soup. It was brought out in Hollohaz porcelain tureen and ladled into porcelain soup bowls that were also made in Hungary.

The second course was cauliflower chicken paprika with cottage cheese noodles, served with Chinese cabbage salad. This course was served on flat plates that had been preheated. There were baskets of freshly baked buns and crusty bread made of rye and wheat. Waiters circled the tables with assorted Hungarian wines.

The third course was stuffed paprika a la Transylvania, again served on preheated plates.

The fourth course was suckling pig baked in a kiln served with celery salad. The pig was on a wooden cutting board and could be sliced into portions according to personal desire.

The dessert was the fifth course - strawberry fantasy torte, fruit tartlets and whisky cake. The cakes were already portioned and sectioned with fancy paper serviettes.

There was champagne. White Riesling and Tokaji on the table. Coffee was from Arabia, tea was from the Orient. The passengers thought they had died and gone to heaven. The young Hungarian man was talking to the chefs and telling them about his good luck at the casino. He had already won 800 dollars.
They didn't believe him.

In the background a Hungarian Tzigany band played a mellow rhapsody on traditional violins with a base and cimbalom.

CHAPTER 5

After dinner, Parker introduced the four Hungarian chefs. They were all from the Hotel Duna Inter-Continental, Budapest, Hungary. Even though most of the passengers were unfamiliar with Hungarian cooking, everyone was delighted with the food. The chefs received a standing ovation. As it turned out, the cakes were the biggest hit.

~

Since the rooms were pre-assigned to everyone, all that remained was to take occupancy. The room numbers corresponded to the numbers on the passenger registration slips. The luggage was already in the rooms.

Although the time was past ten, no one was tired. Nobody wanted to go to bed. Most people could hardly wait to visit the casino and the STORES.

Comparatively, the prices on the garments were one tenth of those on Rodeo Drive. Best of all, the purchases were free. Everyone really liked that part.

Most of the passengers spent their imaginary money on modest outfits except for the two beauticians from Toronto, Lisa Christy, 22 and Karen Kelly, 24. They saw themselves as real movie stars and dressed accordingly. They were quite popular among the unattached young men.

Upon leaving the STORES, people migrated to the casino and started playing blackjack. Everything was on a credit system. The tables had five dollar limits.

A lot of people had never seen the inside of a casino, let alone knew how to play blackjack. Lorraine and Date had played in casinos before, but had never won anything. In fact they had both lost money. For accounting purposes, everyone was encouraged to use their assigned numbers. Expenditures in the casino were recorded and put against the individual's account. There was a free one thousand dollar limit on spending in the casino. There was no limit on the winning.

Lorraine and Date were cautious with their money, especially Date for obvious reasons. Nonetheless they both had the luck of the Irish. Within the hour, Lorraine had already made two hundred and twenty dollars and Date had made two fifty. If they had had more experience they could have made a lot more. There were no pit bosses and the dealers were 'generous'. Since Lorraine had played blackjack before, she was careful not to go overboard with her betting. She got lucky. She was 'up'.

Whenever Parker walked by, he used every opportunity to touch her hand or her arm. He was her 'personal waiter', he said. Each time he touched her, he got a charge, a buzz. It didn't matter whether it was her hand or her finger, even the accidental brush of her dress gave him a never before experienced reaction in his body. This was more than just a 'mother's' touch.

The two beauticians weren't doing too badly either. They were up money too. They were followed by a wall of admirers where ever they went.

As the night wore on, the beauticians needed "smokes" or "soul food." They had used up their last reefer after dinner and a supply of fresh weed looked bleak. Normally drugs of any description were readily available for them whereever they performed. And tonight they missed their regular bar performances. In their "real world "supplies were inexhaustible. They could get drugs anywhere. The twenty five grand looked really good. It would buy a lot of dope. And now the situation was becoming unmanageable. The monkey on their back was restless. They decided to have a meeting. Lisa, being the younger but more aggressive one, grabbed the bull by the horn. She called a meeting in her room with three young men. Evan Jansen, a computer technician; Mike Kevin a farmer and John Matka, who was unemployed.

At the outset of the meeting they were happy and willing participants. Making themselves comfortable in Lisa's spacious room, the three young men and the two dancers got down to some serious communication.

"This is the plan," Lisa began. "I have a cell phone. You guys find a way out of this joint and call this number." She brought up a set of numbers on her I-pod. "Then talk to a guy named Matt. Tell him we are at Eagle Hills Resort. Tell him you are calling for us. Just say you're calling for Lisa and Karen. Tell him we need supplies for two days for five people. Here's two hundred bucks and if he needs more, we'll pay him next time. Cool?"

"Count me out," Evan said.

"What?" Karen jumped up.

"You heard me. I don't do the stuff. You guys go ahead. In fact, I'm out of here right now."

"Hold on Buddy, you're not going to rat on us by any chance are you?" Karen asked with a venomous voice.

"You can rest assured I won't." Evan said matter-of-factly and left the room.

"Asshole" Lisa branded the abstainer and continued,

"Okay then, you two get Matt. You guys know where we are?"

"Yea, sure. We're in a resort."

"I know what you mean" Mike cut in.

"What do I mean?" Lisa asked.

"You were going to tell us that we were on the bottom floor. Right?"

"Holeeee shit. This meeting is over, guys. Let's get out of here. Forget you ever talked to us understand?" Lisa said.
Karen got up too and herded the two 'losers' out the room.

"See ya," she said as she slammed the door behind them.

"Those guys are dumber than three bags of hammers. Have you seen such a bunch of dumb bucks like them before," Lisa asked.

"A real bunch," Karen said pulling out a chair, sitting on it and crossing her legs. "We should have chosen some of the older guys. They have more brains."

"That's exactly why I didn't choose them. They would be too smart. Could cause problems down the road. We'll just have to wing it ourselves. You up to it?"

"Hell, yeah? Let's go." Karen said.

The two moseyed out of the complex through the back door. They walked past the dimly lit swimming pool. Then they tracked over a bulldozed area that had been cleared for more construction.
About two hundred metres ahead they saw some car lights and headed in that direction. Lisa tried her I-pod, but it was still dead. It didn't work because they were still on resort property. Once they reached the paved road and walked up a hundred metres or so, she connected.

Matt the 'druggist' answered. He was familiar with the road that leads to Eagle Hills Resort. He'd be there in an hour exactly, he said.

The girls walked back to Lisa's room and turned on the TV. It was on a repeat time loop, showing details of the resort with some architectural drawings for future developments. They made mixed drinks for themselves and wondered what their life would be like at this resort. They could become Madams... although they would have to learn that new profession. It could be interesting, they thought. Maybe they could get real jobs here... They had to think about that. The minutes dragged on like hours.

~

Matt was an experienced dealer. He knew his business. It might take a little time to drive to the resort, but the effort would pay off in the long run. Especially now that the girls blabbed about a bag of money and the job they might get there. They had the bucks now and had new expensive clothes. He could see himself being fifty grand richer already. The only thing he didn't see, was the tail that had been placed on his behind. And the tail started wagging the minute he left his house.

He had been watched for a long time. All his phones had been bugged and the cops knew where he was every minute. This resort, though, was a brand new location. They had never heard of any purchases from there before. In fact they had no idea what two dancers would be doing there. They were eager to find out. Their job had just started to get interesting.

Major drug dealers were usually handled by the RCMP, and Matt was renowned. Word at headquarters travelled quickly. They knew the location, but why the strippers? Is the resort going to have strippers? Are they having a party?... That's what they had to find out.

When Matt arrived with the goods, the girls were already waiting. He got his two hundred bucks, but three hundred was still owing. He had no problem with the debt, the girls were solid customers.

Matt headed back home but the 'tail' remained. It wagged around the resort a bit but didn't go inside because the security gate was closed. He saw a lot of bright lights and heard some faint music, but that was all.

Grand River Bridge/Flickr- Photo Sharing

CHAPTER 6

E arlier that evening at Union Station in Toronto, the paparazzi had been waiting anxiously for something sensational to occur. It was a busy evening. To keep up with the incredible story, some reporters had been travelling from Brantford to Hamilton and back to Toronto. Yet the most important issue - the abductors identity - was still unknown.

When train #420 pulled into Union Station with almost a third of its passengers missing, it was as sensational as the Toronto Maple Leafs winning the Stanley Cup. Except, of course that was highly unlikely. As the train came to a halt and the passengers disembarked, there were just about as many WRL officials, detectives and press reporters around, as there were travellers. The paparazzi landed on the conductor and the engineer like carrion flies on a three day old road kill. But Kleiner and Bertling were whisked away immediately and the reporters had to settle with talking to the passengers only. The tape and the recorders were extracted from the locomotive and the log book was removed. The train was put on a service line and each coach was screened using a sniffer dog. The locomotive was locked up and the undercarriage checked by a bomb squad. A repair crew was already in Brantford and the severed tab had been found and welded back onto the rail. A taxi cab had been sent for Ed Clement and he was brought to Union Station and immediately rushed into the main office. While some of the WRL managers were tied up in Brantford with McCall and the chief of the Greater Hamilton Police Department, the WRL president and vice president remained at Union Station.

Clement, Kleiner and Bertling and three union reps were ushered into a conference room, where they were joined by some other functionaries from various key departments.

BEWARE
PICKPOCKETS
- AND -
LOOSE WOMEN
NEW ORLEANS POLICE DEPT.

Spittoon

Pot belly stove

Representatives from the Rail Police were also there. The WRL officials were seated by a long table on one side of the room and the train crew along with the union reps on the other. Several technicians with video cameras were in the corner in full view of everyone. The press was not allowed admission.

The room was divided into two camps. Clement's side was laden with anxiety and the other side with suspicion and fear. Had Ed Clement not been sitting, he would have fainted from the immense pressure. Since Kleiner and Bertling had followed instructions to a 'T', they were in a much better position.
Along with the WRL officials was the operations manager who introduced himself as Stetson Skilling. He was going to conduct this interview.

Skilling introduced the top managers and apologized for the 'inconvenience' and started his questioning;

"Mr. Clement, please relax. We are not here to blame anyone. You are all victims of circumstances. This is not a trial, merely an inquiry into the facts, as you yourself have experienced them. We understand that you as well as other train personnel were instructed to do something extraordinary... something you have not done before. Is this correct, Mr. Clement?"

"Yes." Clement answered.

"When this person called you, Mr. Clement, from somewhere..." Skilling drew a semi circle with his right hand, "and asked you to open up the station, what exactly did he say to you?"

"Well, when my phone rang, I picked it up and said hello. The caller also said hello and asked if I was Ed Clement. I answered yes. He went on to say he, he... was calling from the MPO office in Toronto. He told me there was a freight derailment at Two Mile Bridge and would I be good enough to go to the Brantford TH&B station and open it up. He said there would be several buses coming to transfer the passengers to Union Station in Toronto. I asked him when he wanted me to do this. He said, let's see, it's now 6:00 pm. The train will be there at 6:30 or 6:35. Could you leave right now? I said yes sir, I'll be right there."

"Mr. Clement, what were you doing when the phone rang?" Skilling asked, cutting him off impatiently.

"I had just finished supper... and was sitting down to watch the 6:00 o'clock news."

"Was Mrs. Clement at home?"

"Yes, she had just started with the dishes."

"Mr. Clement, I mean... were you not suspicious of the person that called you at your home to open up the station at that hour?"

One of the burly looking union guys stood up and objected to the last question. Skilling apologized and paraphrased the question. "Did you ever get a call from us before?"

"Actually, I did - twice." Clement said and continued, "The first time was when someone from WRL asked me if I would be interested in a caretaker's job and the second time was when someone called from the office about children visiting the station from a local school. They didn't call that late in the evening, though. They called in the afternoon."

Skilling had no knowledge of those communications. Both had occurred before he was appointed to his new job and had no bearing on the present issue at all. He was feeling somewhat confused and turned to the company VP and got the matter verified.

In the meantime, Clement's mind wandered as he tried to recollect the two occasions exactly. Then abruptly he started to speak again, "Yes. I was called from the Personnel Manager's Office the first time and from Public Relations the second time."

The burly union rep leaned towards Clement and advised him not to volunteer any comments unless he was asked. Clement nodded his head.

Skilling, while pausing his questioning, was looking befuddled and was turning red in the face. He thought the union rep said something derogatory about him to Clement. There was a momentary uncomfortable silence in the room. The vice president was whispering something to the person beside him and some of the others were whispering among themselves.

Clearing his throat, Skilling continued. "Okay, Mr. Clement, so then you didn't find anything wrong with that request. What did you think about the derailment? Did you think this was an opportunity for you to make some extra money?"

The burly union rep jumped up and sternly said to Skilling, "Mr. Skilling are you insinuating that Mr. Clement did this for some kind of personal gain? Because if you are... I am going to suggest to Mr. Clement that we get a lawyer. You said you were not going to blame anyone for anything."

Looking Skilling straight in the eye. Clement exploded, "Mr. Skilling, I didn't think of it that way at all. Since the railroad has given me a good life for all the years I worked there, I thought I'd help them out. I would have done that if it was in the middle of the night or in the middle of a snowstorm. I consider myself a loyal employee."

Skilling's face turned red again and his armpits started to sweat. He knew he had to change his mode of questioning. He had to be a little more affable. The vice president stood up and apologized to Clement and instructed Skilling to be more careful with his words. Skilling apologized too and continued:

"So then, Mr. Clement, how far do you live from the station?"

"Just down on Grey Street, about two blocks away." Clement answered.

"So then you walked that distance?"

"I didn't. I drove up. I didn't want to be late. I had to get my uniform out of the closet and it took a little time to get it on. I have gained a few pounds since I last wore it." There was snickering around the room.

"And when you arrived at the station, did you park your car in front of the entrance or did you park it in the parking lot?"

"I parked in the parking lot."

"Then what did you do?"

"I unlocked the door and went in and looked around. Everything was in order, just the way I left it when I was there the last time."

"So then what time did the train get there?"

"6:35, if I remember correctly."

"So then, when the train arrived where were you?"

"I was waiting ten or fifteen minutes for the train by the doorway, and when it arrived I watched Mr. Kleiner and everyone else get off the train. "

"Then what did you do, Mr. Clement?"

"Because there was a light rain falling I said, Listen up, ladies and gentlemen, you might want to come in to wait for the buses. I'll take you on a tour of the waiting room. There's a lot of interesting things inside this station. Then I opened both sides of the front entrance and let the people come inside."

"So then, when the buses arrived, they stopped right at the front door, correct?"

Clement thought for a moment. "There was only one bus and it must have stropped right at the front door. I didn't go outside, I was busy with the passengers."

"So if you didn't go outside and didn't see the bus or the driver, it could have been Saddam Hussein who picked up the passengers, right Mr. Clement?" Loud laughter filled the room.

The burly union rep jumped up again and said, "That's it. We're out of here. Let's go Mr. Clement." The vice president sprung up and said "Please, please... I am going to take over the questioning." But the union reps grabbed Clement by the arm and helped him up off his chair. They were ready to remove him from the room. Shoving and pushing ensued between the union personnel and the WRL people.

"Please gentlemen, please... calm down. We are in a very grave situation. People could be dying. We have an abduction here. We must get to the bottom of this grave matter. Please, Mr. Clement sit down. The vice president pleaded and when he saw the union guys unhanding Clement, he said he was John Brendon, the VP from WRL and he was going to proceed with the questioning.

Rotating his neck nervously, Brendon began, "Mr. Clement... um, did you see the bus driver?"

"Yes,...he, he came in... a younger man, in his thirties, perhaps forty. He had a grey uniform on with a white shirt and black tie. He was about six foot, probably 180 lb. Looked like a clean cut guy, ...oh yeah, he had a uniform hat."

"His face... did you see his face?"

"I did. He was Caucasian, clean shaven, no moustache. He had a tanned face."

"So, then... what did he say to you?"

"He just said that he was in here to pick up a load of passengers and there will be more buses coming shortly."

"Did he say a 'load of passengers' or 'some passengers', Mr. Clement? "

"I thought he said a 'load of passengers'."

Brandon was asking the right questions and got the right answers. But nothing made any sense.

"Did the man say who he was - did he introduce himself to you or to anyone... Did he introduce himself to Mr. Kleiner or to Mr. Bertling and did you tell him who you were?"

Clement was collecting his thoughts. His glance went from Brandon to Kleiner to Bertling. He couldn't remember if he had even said his own name. But he remembered the driver's name, it was Charles Parker. He had heard Parker say that name, he told Brandon.

"Now, did you see him talking to any of the passengers and if he did talk to them, did you hear what he was saying?"

"I... I... didn't hear him talking to the passengers... although he might have been, because he was cherry-picking them. He didn't just take anyone... He pointed to people...selected mostly younger folks."

"Children? Did he take any kids?"

"I don't think so... I...um, I didn't see him take any."

"Women, did he take any women?"

"Yes, but not old women... "

"Did you count how many people he took?"

"No, sir... thirty, I think I heard him say he could only take thirty. I am sorry but I just can't tell you for sure."

Brandon turned to the president and discussed something with him in a hushed voice.

"Mr. Clement, did the passengers take any of their luggage?"

"I didn't see. They must have."

"So, after the bus left with thirty or forty passengers what happened next?"

"After a while, Mr. Kleiner and Mr. Bertling and myself were wondering about the rest of the buses because there didn't seem to be any more coming."

"So then what did you do sir?

"I saw Mr. Bertling go up the locomotive and I guess he tried the rail phone again but still it wasn't working. In the meantime Mr. Kleiner borrowed a cell phone from someone and called the MPO and found out that there was no derailment... nothing. I then used my own cell phone and called 911.

"Then what happened, Mr Clement?"

"A little after seven thirty Captain Rutherford and three other policemen arrived. Later Superintendent McCall called me and told me to stay at the station until he got there. They took the names and addresses of the remaining passengers and around 8:30 superintendent McCall got there and I told him what I just told you. Then the train left for Union Station."

"But Mr. Clement, you told us that you didn't have a phone. How did superintendent McCall talk to you?"

"I had no regular phone, it was disconnected. But luckily I brought my cell phone".

"Did you talk to the police, Mr. Clement?"

"Oh, yes, I talked to both. Captain Rutherford and Superintendent McCall."

"I understand there were reporters there. Did you talk to

them, Mr. Clement?"

"No. Captain Rutherford told me not to."

"Did you talk to anyone else."

"No. None other than the passengers...you know..."

"Did you tell them that there was no derailment?"

"I did to some of them... shouldn't I have?"

"That's okay Mr. Clement. That is all for the moment. Just hang around a little bit longer. We have some snacks on the table outside the door. Go ahead and have whatever you like. There's coffee and other refreshments there too. Please help yourself." Brandon said, straight faced, as he started directing his questioning towards Kleiner.

Aside from some technical questions, Brandon asked the same things as Skilling had asked Clement. In the end everyone thought this was the most incredible event they'd ever heard of.

As the meeting came to an end, Clement was scurried out into a taxi and driven home. Kleiner and Bertling snuck out the back door and Skilling divulged some information to the press similar to the scoop they had got earlier from Chief Stewart in Brantford.

The company president had a violent headache. With great apprehension, he started phoning some directors for an emergency meeting on Saturday. Following that, he and the vice president hastily decided to pay whatever ransom money the abductors asked for.

CHAPTER 7

After grade nine, Lincoln Alexander Hoffmann aka Charles Parker entered university in Hamilton Ontario. Due to his exceptional aptitude in electronics, he was invited to Princeton University where he – like Jeff Bezos - graduated *summa cum laude,* with degrees in engineering. He then went to McMaster where in two short years he graduated in Information Technology and Computer Sciences. By this time, he had made many friends in Silicon Valley. Soon he became one of the top coders and decoders of high computer language. Within another two years, he was regarded as a leading authority in his field in the free world. He developed and advanced lucrative trends in 'cybernetics' and 'nano' technology. He invested the inheritance from his grandfather Gerhard Hoffmann into these technologies.

~

When the Second World War ended, Gerhard Hoffmann, was freed from Auschwitz. A young woman named Adelia was also freed from Block 10. While they were both rehabilitating in Krakow, Poland, Gerhard met Adelia at a movie theatre and they started dating.

Since Adelia showed no physical signs of abuse and since she had only spent a few weeks in Block 10, she thought she was free of any disease. Of course she had no idea what drugs they had given her or what they had injected into her body while she was put to sleep.

At the beginning Gerhard and Adelia lived in separate apartments in the city but they soon fell in love and Adelia moved in with Gerhard. Due to general malnutrition amongst the freed prisoners, they had to be on a strict diet. They didn't have to work anywhere but Gerhard became famous for his knowledge of watches and for his engraving talents. He had set up a small repair shop in their apartment. Adelia was an accomplished musician who played the piano and classical guitar. She played in concerts and taught music to school children during the day and to adults in the evenings. They got married on February the 8th, 1946. The wedding took place at city hall only. Gerhard wanted to have nothing to do with the synagogue or its Rabbi. Oskar Schindler, his long time friend, was his best man.

On November 11, 1947 Adelia had a son and they named him Joseph.

Suddenly in January of 1948 Adelia became ill and within two weeks she was dead from an unknown disease. She died in a Krakow hospital. It was widely believed that her death was due to experiments done on her in Block 10. Gerhard was devastated. He went to Adelia's grave every day and spoke to her for hours. Sometimes he just stood by her grave and cried. He promised he'd never leave her.

The years went by and Joseph started grade school and became a Polish Pioneer (Communist version of Boy Scout). He already spoke three languages. After grade school he went to Teacher's College and when he graduated, he taught German and English to Polish students. All the while Gerhard continued repairing watches and doing his engraving on gold rings and bracelets and numerous other gold items. He also started selling jewellery. His business grew exponentially and he moved downtown to a new location in Krakow and hired some employees.

In 1968, to attend a state function, Joseph went to East Germany. There he met a beautiful girl named Judith. He moved in with her and within a month they were married. Since they were both teachers, they had to teach children communist propaganda that neither one of them believed in.

On December 31, 1970 Alexander was born. Dissatisfied

with the communists in East Germany, the young Hoffmanns decided to flee to West Berlin.

After months of planning, while they were trying to cross a barbed wire barrier on a dark night in 1972, they were both killed when a land mine exploded beneath their feet. Their son Alexander had been left with a babysitter in East Berlin. Had the escape been successful, he would have been taken to West Berlin at a later date. When news of the death of two 'unknown persons' appeared in the East German newspapers, Alexander's babysitter knew exactly who those two people were. She had the unenviable task of giving Gerhard the grim news. Gerhard went to pieces. How much more pain could one person bear in a lifetime, he cried. Then in 1974 his best friend, Oskar Schindler died. He had lost everything to live for in Europe. He applied for Canadian immigration papers and in 1975 he arrived in Canada. He brought Alexander with him, never revealing to anyone, not even to the Canadian authorities, that Alexander was actually his grandson. He added the name 'Lincoln' to Alexander in Canada.

~

By trade, Gerhard was a horologist, who learned his skills in Switzerland in a watch manufacturing factory. Even before the war, he was already a master engraver. He started saving gold cuttings and shavings from jewellery engravings. Pretty soon the cuttings amounted to grams, to decagrams, to kilos. He melted down those cuttings and shavings and sold the gold. He deposited the money into a Swiss account. During the war, because of his masterful engraving talents he worked for top German officials and for Eva Braun. He had to make special jewellery for her, designed by Hitler himself.

He was ordered to engrave printing plates for the wartime German Mark, as well as plates for the illicit American Dollar along with many other fake currencies.

While his work with the most expensive Swiss watches like Rolex, Oister or Mando Blanco, was unprecedented, his

79

engraving work was legendary. Some of his work is displayed even today in museums in Europe.

As Hitler intensified his genocide against the Jews, Gypsies and many others that didn't fit his scheme, Gerhard too was sent to Auschwitz where he worked directly for Adolf Eichmann. He was already friends with Oskar Schindler, the ambitious industrialist and humanitarian.

In Auschwitz, Gerhard had a secret rite of passage - a set of instantly recognizable numbers tattooed on his forearm. This special number designated him as a privileged Jew. He was privileged because of his essential and sensitive work for the German government. His work included altering names on confiscated gold jewellery and various religious gold items. Luckily, even in the concentration camp he was able to save the gold shavings and cuttings. Almost all of that gold, went to his friend Schindler, who used the money to bribe German officials and to buy freedom for many of his Jewish workers.

Gerhard also had one of the most sickening jobs in the camp. He had to watch as gold teeth were extracted from gassed corpses. The dentist who carried out this atrocity was a tall, strong, dark haired man who never spoke. The Germans called him "die taube Zahnfee" (the mute Tooth Fairy).

Both Gerhard and a Jewish guard had to count and log the extracted teeth and their two sets of numbers had to match. They were also in charge of shipping. The gold teeth had to be packed with special markings on the boxes and the shipments were always picked up by couriers direct from the Fatherland.
When the war ended, the guard and the 'Tooth Fairy' disappeared without a trace. Gerhard always wondered what happened to the men and the shipments of gold teeth.

~

In Canada, Gerhard was determined to forget the past and spent his energy guiding Alexander through his formative years.

Gerhard continued engraving and the shavings kept accumulating.

As gold became more valuable the shavings came to be worth a lot of money. And there was no tax on the shavings... because no one knew they even existed. Since he was the only authorized Rolex repair person in Canada, his popularity grew and his wealth grew as well. Gerhard moved again into another new location, and hired more employees. Even though the Rolex watches were the most expensive watches in the world, young Alexander wasn't interested in them or in the engraving or in the jewellery Gerhard sold. Alexander did other things.

After Lincoln Alexander finished university, earlier than most, he invested in cybernetics and his investments began paying off big time. He channelled the better part of his money into exciting new concepts. One of them, and the most ambitious, was the Eagle Hills Project. Even at a young age he recognized the potential of that area.

Alexander had no interest in Gerhard's business. As Gerhard aged and his sight failed, he sold it to his right hand man. Meanwhile, Alexander formed an international company and made the Eagle Hills Project a reality.

~

Gerhard Hoffmann became ill suddenly and died in 1999, at the age of 89. The numbers tattooed on his forearm had been his 'rite of passage' and they later became his Swiss bank account number.

On his death bed he said, "Son, I was a very religious person before the war but I will never forgive a God that let millions die in Auschwitz. I'll never forgive the God that let your grandmother suffer in Block 10. I'll never forgive the God that could have prevented the entire Second World War and didn't. Promise me that you'll always be true to your race."

Alexander vowed that as long as he lived, he'd be true and help the poor and downtrodden. He'd always look at life as a present, as a gift.

81

    "I'll pass these words along to my children and tell them to pass them along to theirs," Alexander said as he bid his father goodbye. "Shalom Aleichem, Father (Peace be with you, Father)."
    And as he lay dying, Gerhard whispered, "Shalom, son."

CHAPTER 8

Late Friday evening the activities at the Eagle Hills Resort started to catch up with Lorraine. Even though she was winning at the blackjack table, she had had enough of the casino and prepared to call it a night. Lorraine would have wanted to chat with Parker a little more, but he seemed nervous or aloof. He had helped her with the cards, brought her drinks but never engaged in any meaningful conversation. When they talked, they talked only business. He was right on the money and was precise when he talked about banking; but the minute the conversation turned personal, he was uneasy, almost shy. She bid him goodnight. He didn't look quite right to her.

"See you tomorrow," he said quietly, almost uncertainly.

She went to her room and threw herself onto the bed. She would have fallen asleep in an instant had Parker not been on her mind. He was a very interesting person, articulate, intelligent and smart. Wealthy for sure. He was definitely not married. Eccentric obviously. Judging by this unusual situation he had to be. Then she thought of her vacation next week...and McCall. Chance started to feel like an old shoe... what would he be like as a husband, or as a father to her children? Would he want any kids? It seemed he didn't even want to get married. There must be someone out there that would appreciate her more than Chance! She couldn't remember the last time she stayed up this late, gambling no less, alone, no less. She started to enjoy her freedom, her independence. Relentlessly, Parker kept creeping back into her mind.

She felt excited about her winning but for the life of her she couldn't figure out why he was so attentive, yet not saying much. There were other women around who were at least as attractive as she was if not more so. People with money can do anything they want, she thought. Maybe this is a new trend. Maybe this is a new way to hire good people. Maybe he thinks she is special. She should be, a bank manager would be even more special! Maybe he doesn't want to get too friendly. The abduction didn't make too much sense. However, if he wanted to make a lasting impression, it did. But whenever he was with her, he always appeared somewhat anxious and nervous. She stifled a yawn, undressed and went in the bathroom and turned on the shower. As she walked by the splashing shower she pulled the curtain closed. She glanced at her image in the mirror and smiled approvingly. She had a beautiful body. Eat your heart out Chance, she thought as she remembered a cute line in a book: 'a woman's alter ego is the favourite image of herself.' This was her favorite image.

After the shower had refreshed her, she thought about going back to gamble a little more, but chose not to. She opened the bar fridge and got herself a pop and drank half of it thinking, there will be another day tomorrow.

The bed felt good even without McCall in it. But then, she thought... why hasn't he given me a ring? What is the hold up? She wasn't getting any younger and wanted a family. The song about not finding a large enough diamond didn't wash with her anymore and it was becoming a lame excuse. Was there someone else? Or was he scared of marriage? Or was he too lazy? Lazy... probably. These things were not clear to her and they bothered her greatly. While thinking of him and of Parker and of the good time she was having, she fell asleep.

CHAPTER 9

Thinking about Frank Adams and the abduction, Chance McCall couldn't fall asleep until well past three am, and he awoke from his nightmarish dream at ten minutes after six on Saturday morning. He was thrashing Hoffmann in the water and when he opened his eyes he was relieved it was just his pillow not Hoffmann's neck he was twisting. He couldn't believe he woke up so early. He shivered. What a dream, he thought and he was glad it was over. His stomach started to growl so loud he was afraid it might wake up the neighbours. It was way too early. He had to have more sleep. Then his stomach growled again so he got up and looked in the fridge for something edible other than butter and onions. There was nothing appetising. He wished he was at his girlfriend's place because she always had some snacks in her fridge. He turned off the lights and fell back into bed. Outside it was still dark and in his room a neon light irritated the hell out of him. He got up and closed the gap in the curtains and then went back to bed again. Now the neon sign reflection was on the ceiling. He buried his head in the bedcovers until he couldn't breathe anymore. He tossed and turned a few times more and counted backwards from one hundred. He even counted sheep for the third time - black sheep, this time. Nothing worked.
He got up again, took a shower, got dressed and left his apartment. He went to the corner all night eatery and had breakfast. After he finished his coffee he started to feel as if he'd had a full night's sleep. He took the elevator to his car in the

parking garage and drove to the station. The night sergeant smiled at him and asked him if he'd just come back or if he hadn't even gone home yet. Judging by the number of phone calls, it was going to be a crazy day, and he should get some rest, the sergeant said. Suddenly McCall realized he didn't look as good as he thought he did. Nonetheless he told the sergeant he had been home already but couldn't fall asleep. He asked him if anything had happened in the short time he was away. The sergeant said he hadn't heard anything from the patrols or anyone else, but there had been constant phone calls from reporters. And he was sorry to hear about Frank. McCall sighed.

He went into his office and contrary to his white lie to the chief last night, the cleaners were just finishing off and the floor was still damp. Through the pleasant smell of floor wax he could still detect cigar smoke in the air. The cleaning man and his wife passed by his office again and asked if he wanted his door closed. He said no, he just wanted to keep it ajar. He was hoping the cigar smoke would dissipate a little faster if the door was left open, he told them. He read his notes from last night and agreed with every word he had written. It was all true and there was nothing more he could add. He even had the right 'clues' highlighted. The abductors were still unknown and that was impossible to believe. He had to get something going. Instinctively, he started planning his day. He remembered he was in a different capacity today. Today he was the 'deputy dog'. He put Lorraine at the top of the list. He had to find out where she was. That was priority one. He ran his finger down yesterday's list of places he'd called and highlighted the ones that were supposed to get back to him today. There were four places he had to hear from and he marked those with a purple accent highlighter. He checked the answering machine – nothing. There were some junk E-mails nothing else. He had no messages from anyone. He visualized himself in Adam's shoes and tried to think like a deputy chief. It was easier said than done. He knew one thing for sure, if he was going to survive in this position, he'd better start thinking like a deputy chief.

He asked his staff for the composite drawing of the bus driver. Then he double checked to make sure the license plate number, the registration and VIN numbers were correct, and had been sent to all the OPP headquarters. He made sure the RCMP and CSIS had them as well. He also e-mailed everything to the chief. His phone was ringing every five minutes and it wasn't even seven-thirty yet. Now his secretary Louise was calling him and asking if he wanted to talk to some reporters. He told her no. He didn't need to speak with any reporters.

As the uniformed officers started trickling in, everyone was talking about the 'Mystery Bus' and Frank Adams. To ease the load on the desk sergeant, he phoned Zelda Sams himself at her house and asked her to come in to take all the WRL related calls and handle the press. He was going to have his hands full just managing the uniformed officers.

He studied the missing persons list and was surprised to see there were only a dozen or so names on it. Of course, there would be some people on the train who wouldn't be missed until Monday morning when they didn't show up for work.

The bus driver's MO had been nailed down. He wondered however, if any of the 'left over' passengers had additional information about those who were taken, but he doubted that. He called Captain Rutherford's office and requested the names, addresses and phone numbers that had been collected on those remaining passengers and left a message for him to be available for a meeting on short notice.

The phone rang again. It was a civilian by the name of Baird Jones, Louise said. He apparently had information about some unusual activity on the railroad track last night. McCall talked to Jones and jotted down his phone number and thanked him for the information. Jones asked if he was eligible for any monetary reward. McCall told him he didn't know, but would find out and have someone call him back. Jones asked McCall when, because he could really use the money right now. He told Jones again that someone would get back to him today or tomorrow. Money, money, money. That's all people can think about nowadays, he murmured to himself. But he had to hand it to the guy for his precise recollection. He had been out walking his dog when he saw two guys in coveralls and hard hats working on the rails with a cordless grinder. He had been observant enough to know the difference between a grinder and a saw. As for the men in coveralls - they could have been just about anybody. He never saw their faces, Jones had told him. When McCall asked Jones how he knew that it was a fake derailment, Jones said he had heard it on the evening news. McCall was amazed how fast Jones had connected what he'd seen with the evening news. And he called the workers 'gandy dancers.' He had to look up what gandy dancers meant on the internet. Apparently the railroad maintenance people were called that. At least he'd learned a new word.

He called the hospital and inquired about Frank Adams. He was told Adams was in a coma and moribund. McCall felt sorry for Adams and his family. He had hoped Frank would recover, but knew in his heart this wasn't going to happen. To add to everyone's sorrow, a new grandson had just been born.

He thought about calling Lorraine's head office in Vancouver but decided not to. Instead he called her apartment and when her answering machine came on he just said,

"Hi, hon. I'm checking in on you again in case you've been trying to get a hold of me. I'm just worried about you."

At the end of his shift the desk sergeant rang McCall one last time and said, "The chief is inquiring if there is anything new. I told him that you were in, that was new, and he answered that if that was the case he wanted to talk to you."
McCall pushed line two. The chief asked him what he was doing in so early. McCall told him he hadn't been able to sleep all night. The chief asked him why he hadn't tried some hot milk.

McCall changed the subject.

He told Stewart about the tipster. The chief didn't think Jones was a big deal since one could easily figure out how to cut a metal tab with a grinder. That of course wasn't the point. The point was knowing the difference between a saw and a grinder.

"If the man had seen their faces it would be a different story," the chief said and continued, "We only have two detectives so you better let them handle the next-of-kin of the known passengers. That allows the uniformed officers to remain on patrol." He reminded McCall to compare notes with everyone at the next meeting. Other than that, whatever he decided was fine with him. He was on his way to visit Frank Adams at the hospital and would come in later. Before hanging up he added in a threatening tone, "Don't screw up!" McCall pretended to be shaking in his boots. The chief liked to act tough. He acted tough and he looked tough. He was a big barrel-chested guy and everyone knew he was tough.

When he had his cap on, it looked like he had a full head of hair but, without it, the bald spot in the middle of his head was readily visible. He had a large scar on that bald spot. The scar had been caused by a sharp rock in the waters of Cabo San Lucas when he dove into the water a little too close to the rocks. He said he didn't die because he was quite drunk. They all were, many years ago during March break at University.

A fax came into McCall's office from Captain Rutherford. It listed the names of the 'left over' train passengers. He started studying the names hoping to find someone famous or wealthy. No one stood out. He was also expecting a call from central command and from the Special Task Force when a thought occurred to him and left him in a cold sweat. What if the abductors start knocking people off and sending bodies out to make their point. But what was their point? What if-what if... he was full of what ifs. Who, who were these abductors?

He went for a coffee. There wasn't any made yet so he started looking for the ingredients when Louise arrived to help. She said she would look after the coffee as it was not an easy thing to make. He asked her why and she explained that she used bottled water because coffee made with tap water tasted like swamp sludge. He didn't know that. To him it wouldn't have made any difference. Coffee was coffee. She promised to bring him a cup when it was ready. He told her he wanted it black this time, no sugar and he was really looking forward to it ASAP. She grimaced and smiled. He hoped the coffee would revitalize his thinking process.

The two detectives arrived and started talking shop right away. McCall told them Frank Adams was near death and he had been appointed interim deputy chief. They acted amazed and wanted to know how to address him now. He tried to look tough like the chief and said, "Just call me Your Highness." He asked them to be in the conference room at eight. He called WRL and had a short conversation with Skilling and Brandon and neither had anything new to suggest or add. They had analyzed the false MPO's tape a dozen times and the composite drawing meant nothing. The most important thing everyone was waiting for, hadn't happened. There was no ransom demand. Nobody knew what to do next.

Rail Connector

CHAPTER 10

A s McCall was heading to the conference room Louise intercepted him with his coffee. He almost collided with her because his mind was on the kidnapped passengers. Even though it was Saturday, everyone was working overtime. No one knew exactly why except that something big was in the offing and when it happened everyone had to be ready. But nothing was happening and nothing kept on happening. McCall was really searching for something brilliant to say to his men. This was the first time in his life he had gone to a briefing with a confused mind.

The officers too had to say something positive to the grieving parents or relatives, but what. He had instructed them to say something pacifying and to remind people to look at the bright side. That this is Canada. Canada does well with radical groups. The abductors will ask for money and they will be paid. This is a domestic situation. Some officers, however, knew of incidents that hadn't turned out too well. McCall reminded them that there had been no sign of violence and no one had been hurt.

After the briefing McCall sent some officers to gather information from Captain Rutherford's list and sent the detectives to talk to the next of kin of the known abducted passengers. All others he sent to check on the back roads.

No one had snickered or cracked any jokes. Everyone figured this was the calm before the storm. They all went out to do their job with a heavy feeling in their hearts.

~

As McCall got back in his office he leafed through some tabloids and newspapers Zelda had brought in.

The chief was right on the front page of 'On The Spot', the local daily newspaper.

This will make him fume, he thought. The chief hated publicity. Actually he hated bad publicity. He liked good publicity but that was hard to come by these days, and this... this was not good. This was bizarre publicity. The paper quoted his report from last night word for word. The paper also said that the other rags around the world are calling this the 'TH&B Case.' And most papers were spelling it out: the 'To Hell and Back Case.' Emphasizing HELL and BACK.

The abduction rippled through the nation and beyond. The Prime Minister at 24 Sussex had to take two sleeping pills before he went to bed last night, one of the papers had reported.

From the unbelievable to the bizarre, the world newspapers wrote the most imaginative bits of news:

The CP (Canadian Press) reported the possible awakening of home grown terrorists. The NAP (North American Press) blamed an unknown terrorist group. The European Press (EP) sided with the Canadian theory. None could suggest a solution and none could second guess the abductors. Everyone felt sorry for the abducted passengers and their families. Then, of course there were always the usual obnoxious tabloids with their take on the case.

The most outrageous was the British tabloid, THE TRUTH IS, which wrote: "We always knew something like this was going happen only we didn't know when and where. Recently discovered aliens on the moon were marginalized to the point where they couldn't take it anymore. They said enough is enough. They called upon other long ignored and grossly dissatisfied third class intergalactic inhabitants to unite. The Moonies, being the closest to the Earth, got the first opportunity of removing a bus load of Earthlings from the population. This is just the beginning. There will be more abductions in the near future. If you are a human, you are advised to stay indoors and avoid mass transportation!"

Quick-thinking moped manufacturers, bicycle makers, single passenger car makers were already gearing up for large scale one person vehicle production. Families consisting of more than three were told to break up because it was too risky to have more than three people together. Large church memberships were a thing of the past. Their spiritual leaders were forced to engage members singularly. Sport stadiums were closed. Wrestling matches were cancelled and social gatherings were postponed. There was even a picture with the story, showing a bus unloading people on the Moon who were given shovels and made to dig for water.

The main American tabloid called the PLANETARY POT, (Planetary Paper Of Today) was not as detailed. It reported:

"Bus load of Canadian travellers kidnapped by sex-crazed Zombies and taken to an undisclosed location where they were water-boarded. Once the gender of the passengers was confirmed some were shipped to Zambonia and others to some sexually underdeveloped nations that aren't even on the map. At this point the ransom amount is not specified, but we think it will be a doozy, most likely millions of dollars worth of narcotics."

One picture showed ordinary people lying on seats in a bus, bombed out of their minds. The writing under the picture is either in Zambonian, or some yet undiscovered language. It appears to be undecipherable.

Undecipherable, just like this case is. No one could understand why there was still no demand for ransom. People

93

started to believe the tabloids. For the first time ever, no terrorist group, no rogue country was claiming the abduction.

~

McCall's phone rang. And every time it did, he hoped it would be Lorraine. With trepidation, he picked it up. It was Louise. She wanted to know if he was interested in talking to Marcel Le Febvre, the RCMP Commissioner in Ottawa. Or should she tell him to wait until the chief came in. McCall told her it made no difference. Neither one of them knew anything more than what had happened yesterday. He took the call.

He pushed line one. Commissioner Le Febvre introduced himself and told him he had heard about Frank Adam's heart attack and he expressed his regret. While he was concerned about the passengers, he had no suggestions as to where to go to find them. They talked for a long time, exchainging words of disbelief at the abduction. He said the nation was ready, in fact the whole world was ready for the worst. The Canadian Security Intelligence Service (CSIS), the FBI, the KGB had no prior warning or the faintest clue. He asked McCall to let him know immediately if anything happened. McCall assured him he would be one of the first to know and hung up.

Since there was no information from WRL or any Ontario Provincial Police detachments, there wasn't much else he could do for the case. He was racking his brain for an idea. He could hardly wait for the chief to come in and was looking at the clock constantly. He studied the artist's conception of the bus driver again, and the picture was totally meaningless to him, with or without the cap. Later, when Clement, Kleiner, and Bertling saw it, they all agreed the artist's rendition was pretty good.

~

McCall turned on the TV in his office and searched for a news station and got CNN. Then he flipped to CBC. They already had the artist's picture and the description of the driver. Now that was a surprise, they must have gotten the information from head office. He switched to CNN although he wouldn't have needed to, since he couldn't imagine a bus load of people entering through US customs without passports. He channel surfed and finally settled with CBC again and caught the regular anchor person discussing the abduction of a boat load of people from Syria. There were two hardened reporters sitting at the table and they both agreed abducted people didn't have to be rich or famous. The important thing was that they were in good shape. They didn't want to bother with sick people.

Everything started to make sense. That was a good clue. The bus driver selected younger persons only! That could be a very important part of this abduction. Of course Canada is far from Syria or the Mediterranean sea, but...one could never tell... Canada had some pretty radical groups too. For instance, the environmentalists, the animal life activists, the various dissatisfied religious groups, to name a few. Money doesn't always have to be the centre of a demand.

He thought it might not be a bad idea to get some knowledgeable people together and get a round table discussion going. He looked at the time, as he had done so often in the last dozen hours, and it was almost 10:30. The chief could still be a couple of hours away.

Just to get going on this idea of his, he started to think about some people he could invite to this discussion. He jotted down some names. They could have the meeting at the TV station, in-camera or perhaps even live on TV. That would give the chief some positive exposure. He would like that. They could have Captain Rutherford there too.

He started to feel better. He felt like he was earning his salary now. He wrote down what was already known and speculated on what they might find out. He put the emphasis on the latter. He got Louise to start phoning some TV stations.

~

Being a Saturday, it was apparent that most of the people he'd suggested for the round table discussion were not available. But leave it to Louise. She produced some others just as knowledgeable, or maybe even more so, than the ones he had chosen. Of course they would have to involve WRL. However, he felt their input would be minimal, since they were the victims.

If the discussion were going to be televised, he thought early in the afternoon would be a good time to start the taping for the evening news. Since Louise had chosen CBC in Toronto as the host, their offices would be nearby. He called WRL and told them what he was planning.

WRL was delighted with the idea and suggested one of their security people come along.

He called the chief's house and spoke to Margaret and asked her to have the chief call him when he got home from the hospital, before he left for the office. He then asked her to get the chief's good uniform ready, perhaps his medals as well because he was going to be on TV. She got all excited. McCall told her that he himself wouldn't be on TV, only the chief. He blushed when she remarked that he was better looking than the chief. McCall was no slouch. He was 5'11",180 lbs. and had dark curly hair and a moustache. Lorraine thought he was cute.

He stopped admiring himself. He began to think however, that perhaps the chief might want to send him into the spotlight In that case he'd better start worrying about his own uniform... and medals... if... if he had any. He had some... but where?

The phone rang! Lorraine...? No.
"Good thinking, McCall. I am coming in to talk to you... but, I want you to go to the discussion. Get your feet wet. I'm not in the right frame of mind anyway. Poor Frank is not good. The doctors are giving him a maximum of a couple of days. His wife is with him right now and I don't think he is aware of what's going on"

As McCall's mind flip-flopped between the interview and Frank's condition, he could imagine how the chief must be feeling. He was about to lose his right hand man, had his wife seething over her brother's 140 dollar fine and had a busload of abducted passengers to boot.

McCall's stomach was letting him know that a little food would go a long way. All he had had was cold coffee. The phone rang again. Margaret was calling this time to say Frank had just passed away. He almost fell off his chair. She said he didn't die alone, that his wife Edith had been by his side all day. She held his hand and stroked his arm. His arm was colder than ice, Edith said and his mouth was open. He looked very peaceful though. The wrinkles on his forehead smoothed, and his face looked artificial, pale, she said. He had been hooked up to intravenous and some other wires. Margaret was sobbing.

~

Earlier at the hospital, Edith had not taken her eyes off Frank... and then he was gone. She kissed him on the cheek gentler than ever, and said, "My dear Frank, you never said goodbye... what am I going to do now?" Then she looked at the monitor on the wall showing an electronically generated flat line. The line came from infinity and went to infinity. And she said,
    "That is how long I am going to love you... forever.

~

After McCall swallowed the lump in his throat he pulled himself back to reality. He thought it was imminent that the chief would be thinking of him... as a deputy chief.

"Aint that a bummer. As if we didn't have enough problems, now Frank is gone," he said to himself as he went to get a coffee. Actually, he needed more than just a coffee, he needed a Tylenol. Actually, he needed more than a Tylenol, he needed a shoulder to cry on or an understanding soul to speak to.

And he thought of Lorraine. There comes a time when we all need someone. Sorrow is easier to accept when it is shared, he thought.

CHAPTER 11

The meeting was to be held on the 16th floor at the CBC building. He had to be there by 3:00pm. The taping was going to be live with a thirty second delay for editing purposes. Before he went, he wanted to hear his chief's take on this mess and his point of view.

When the chief showed up at the office at 12:30, neither one of them said anything about Frank, they just hugged each other and in a tremulous voice McCall started asking the chief a few things that were important to him and things he wanted to relay to the public.

"Look, I want people to view this abduction as a very serious matter." The chief started, clearing his throat. "To the public it might appear that the police are not doing anything about this unprecedented case. We are. We are doing what we can. We are ready to face any situation and we are waiting for the abductors to reveal themselves. Other than that, you have to stress the point that we want to hold up our good image as hard working civil servants, successful, result oriented, go-by-the-book people. We live by and protect the laws of the land and we work hand in hand with any political party that is in command. We don't complain and we don't brag. We achieve our goals. We work with our community and we innovate where we can. We're professionals. We do our job efficiently and diligently. We are willing to listen but our most important objective is order and safety. We will not rest until this case is solved, whether it is tomorrow, a day later, or a week later."

To McCall, the chief started to sound like his mom, God rest her soul. Of course... he didn't tell the chief that. He just said,

"I understand, Chief."

Stewart asked McCall to phone him when he was done with the meeting and he said he would. The chief said he'd look after things while he was gone. He knew the chief just wanted to be alone to reminisce about Frank.

He gathered up some notes and headed home. While he was going to his car, he glanced at the sky. It was clear and blue. The only thing that appeared different was the number of vapour trails. Were they being made by jets looking for the 'mystery bus'? he wondered, as he drove to his favourite eatery for lunch. Then he went up to his apartment.

~

In the back of his dresser drawer, he found his hard earned badges and pinned them onto his uniform. He picked up his folder and left the apartment. He arrived at the CBC station at 2:30 and they appreciated that he had come early because they had forgotten to tell him he needed makeup. He objected to the makeup part and said he wasn't a woman. They laughed. The makeup was necessary. Without makeup people are expressionless. Even though he felt uncomfortable, he grudgingly complied.

~

A couple of professors arrived from U of T (University of Toronto) along with a sharply dressed middle aged woman from a well known law firm in Toronto and a man from WRL.The moderator was an experienced newscaster, a very pleasant man.

They were set up in a studio, with lights all over the place. Cameras were aimed at them from every direction. There was an audience, just a handful of people sitting in the gallery, most of them were part of the taping crew.

The moderator introduced McCall to the TV audience stating his rank and his role as the key investigating officer in this abnormal abduction case.

After McCall outlined the circumstances and disseminated the information, the professors with their mathematical equations and parallel theories, went off on a tangent. They talked a lot but didn't say too much. The lady appeared to be the most intelligent person with her comments. She asked McCall if he had ever thought of some company wanting to experiment with a product like a drug, or some sort of brain washing or mind-altering procedure? She smiled and said it was a farfetched idea, but so was this situation. He had to agree with her on that. All in all, it had been a productive debate and he was sure the audience was sufficiently mystified to keep them glued to their TV. The professors will now have something spectacular to teach next week and the networks will have another prime time money maker, because today this 'mystery bus' case was the biggest thing in the world.

When he got back to his office, the chief was still there. He was talking to some of the uniformed officers discussing the experiences they had had with the passengers they had interviewed. Most comments were personal opinions, implying that they were happy it wasn't any of their relatives who had been kidnapped.

The detectives McCall had sent to talk to the next of kin of those abducted were not back yet. Their reports were the most important ones to him.

As he was planning to remain at the station until he got really tired, he asked the chief if he wanted to go out for dinner. The chief thought it was a good idea. He called Mrs. Stewart and told her that the two of them were going out to eat. She said she was already cooking and was making something McCall liked; stuffed turkey thighs with creamed spinach and mashed potatoes.

The chief told McCall all this and from behind a thick cloud of cigar smoke he asked, "What do you want to do. Do you want to come over?"

McCall was licking his chops already and said, "sure".

~

"Dinner will be around seven" the chief said. McCall knew Chief Stewart wanted to go home and suggested he just go, as he had had a long day. They all had. Besides he thought, he'd already had his soaking in the chief's toxic cigar fumes. He told Stewart those cigars would kill him, if they didn't kill him first. The chief said he didn't inhale. He believed the chief like he believed in the Easter Bunny.

~

At 5:10 the first detective Mike Pucci came back to the office with a long face. This was about the toughest assignment he'd ever had, he said. McCall agreed. Pucci said his first visit took him to Cynthia Livingstone's parents in Toronto. While at the University of St. Thomas, Cynthia was an honour student and she had a guaranteed job opportunity at a St. Thomas auto maker's engineering department. She was coming home with her boyfriend Stephen Klint to celebrate her birthday. Klint was from London, Ontario and was also an engineering student. Pucci suggested to Cynthia's parents that this might be a case where people were retained for something other than money. He couldn't tell what that other reason was or who the abductors were. He just had that gut feeling and for that reason, he encouraged them to just wait, just hang in there. The abductors would have to reveal themselves soon. They couldn't carry thirty people around as that would just slow them down. They will identify themselves and make their demands. Perhaps they're looking to get some concessions such as a reduced sentence or someone's release from jail. Pucci tried to pacify Cynthia's parents to no avail. He told them the police were ready to act as soon as the abductors

102

revealed their identity, but he didn't think his reasoning had made any impact. He couldn't settle them down at all. Everybody wanted to know who these abductors were. That of course Pucci couldn't tell them. Klint's parents in London felt the same way.

Pucci then he went to Diana Markle's parents. They couldn't believe that she was one of the abducted persons. Diana's mother had been talking to her on the bus when the line went dead. They couldn't call her back or anything. That was a mystery. Her parents were expecting her at the Union Station at 8:00pm. Everyone was there but their daughter. Pucci told them there were thirty people in all missing. That of course was of no comfort to them. Pucci said Diana was just coming home for a visit. She worked as a veterinarian in St. Thomas.

"Did you say her phone went dead," McCall asked.

"Yeah... They tried to call her a dozen times and they couldn't connect," Pucci said and continued, "I tried to call her too, but to no avail. I couldn't connect either."

"The battery must have died in her cell, eh" McCall said.

"Yeah," Pucci agreed and went on, "Once I told them we hadn't heard anything from the abductors, it became impossible to put anyone at ease." He said he'd make out his report tomorrow or Monday.

The other detectives, Peter Wilde came in with a different story.

Peter went to see a Mr. and Mrs. Varga whose nephew Imre was coming to visit them from Windsor. This fellow Imre was a 25 year old male living at Mrs. Varga's sister's place in Windsor. "Imre doesn't speak English very well because he is from Budapest, Hungary. He is also a diabetic and they think he's got enough medication with him but he could still be in a tough situation," Peter said as he looked questioningly at McCall.

"Hungarians are pretty tough people so I wouldn't worry about him. The freedom fighters got rid of the Russians. Maybe he'll free everyone from the abductors too," McCall said.

"Are there other nationalities amongst those kidnapped? Let's just take a quick look." Peter suggested. All the other names appeared to be English.

~

As it was about time for McCall to leave for the chief's house, he said goodbye to his men and told them to keep their ears open tomorrow even though it was Sunday. They asked if they could wear jeans if they were called in.

"You can wear skirts if you want," he joked even though he was as bitter as he could be.

~

McCall needed a stiff drink and a beer to chase his blues away. He was certain that with Adam around, the chief would have both of those drinks available.

He left the station at 6:30 but told his sergeant he'd be back. He said that in the same way as Schwarzenegger said in a certain movie.

~

At the chief's house McCall had his drinks and they had their dinner. The "To Hell and Back" segment about the Mystery Bus hadn't aired. It had been put off until 10:00pm. They were sitting around the table discussing Frank and the impact this kidnapping had had on the various families. It had to be unbearable for the ones affected. Just like the situation with Lorraine was for him.

"What can people do when the police can't help them?" McCall asked.

"Who do the police go to," the chief replied. Nobody had an answer.

McCall told the chief that he had called in another operator to help with the phone calls. There were tons of inquiries streaming in constantly. That many calls would have been too much for the night sergeants to handle. The chief agreed.

He was about to thank Margaret for the stellar dinner when the phone rang. The chief picked up the phone. It was Frank's wife Edith, who wanted to talk to Margaret. Frank was a very close family friend to the Stewarts, and was godfather to the chief's first son. No question about it, Frank was everyone's friend. McCall had learned a lot from Frank. He had been like a father not just to him, but to all of the officers.

He thanked Margaret for the delicious dinner and with a heavy heart he headed back to the office. Mike Pucci and some other officers were still there. They were in the lunch room eating Kentucky Fried Chicken. They had put it on company expense because they were doing overtime. McCall had authorized this because it was in their contract and they were indeed doing overtime. He took a copy of the list of missing passengers and asked the officers to come into the conference room for a meeting. They said they would be in after they finished eating.

While waiting, he placed the list of the known passengers on the projector along with their addresses, occupations and all the other available information. Everyone was from a different walk of life. The average age was thirty two. He didn't see any relationship connection to high profile persons or celebrities, only boyfriends, girlfriends, husbands and wives. The oldest person was 58 his name was George Date and he was from St. Thomas, his daughter-in-law had reported. All the others were either going on vacation, visiting someone or just coming home from somewhere.

As the officers came in, they admired his professionally created list and praised him for his computer skills. He thanked them kindly and bookmarked the list. They discussed the list briefly. He said he hoped something interesting would be added to it tomorrow. Then in tough-talk again, he told them to go home and let the regular duty officers carry on. But be available on short notice. One officer said, Thank you, Your Excellency, as he had forgotten that McCall had told them to address him as 'Your Highness'.

He was glad some of the uniformed officers agreed to come in tomorrow if they were needed. The best they could do for the time being was to fly by the seat of their pants, try to pacify and console the unfortunate parties, and apologize for not having any more information. What else could they do? They already had every highway, every side road, every street, every parking lot every empty building checked, all to no avail. They were now starting to check bus depots, trailer parks, commercial truck depots and abandoned barns. They had checked lanes leading to ponds, lakes and rivers. They had checked the canyons along with canals and the Niagara Gorge. They had contacted the native reserves to inquire about any unusual activity. Most officers ran out of business cards and in those instances they had to leave their phone numbers on pieces of paper.

According to newspaper articles, some politicians were trying to score points by blaming the police, while others were sympathizing with them. The Prime Minister was asking for calm. The police had put as much information on the internet as they could and hoped for some kind of lead from somewhere. McCall was checking his e-mails constantly, nothing. Everyone was simply speculating. There was nothing tangible to go on. Judging by the number of phone calls, this detachment had to be the busiest place on earth and he was beginning to go out of his mind. He thought about visiting some of his regular night spots. Sometimes, by chance, he got good information there. First though, he wanted to go home to listen to his answering machine and change into civilian clothes.

~

It was 9:30 when he stopped at 'The Air-Port', a popular night spot in Toronto. He was just in time to see the tail end of a fist fight outside. It must have started at the bar he thought, because the manager had swung open the door and grabbed a guy to pull him back in while shouting at him, "Look, you broke the bloody table. You're paying for it." Then three police cars

106

arrived. There was another man sitting on the curb bleeding from the mouth and blotting blood from his lips with a tissue.

As McCall was entering the bar, an officer started shoving him aside. McCall was in no mood to argue and got tough with the cop. He showed him his badge and announced his rank. That put the young policeman in his place in a hurry and he quickly opened the door and kept it open for McCall to mosey in, apologizing all the while. McCall told him it was okay, and sat down on a high bar stool.

He didn't have to wait too long before a bearded man sitting beside him started talking about the 'To Hell and Back' case. McCall could hardly wait to hear what his story was going to develop into. The bearded man said his co-worker had inside information. "This is the work of a home grown terrorist group," he said.

McCall joined the conversation just to find out what group he was referring to. The man didn't know exactly but said he heard some religious sect in Toronto was involved. He would be finding out more about this on Monday. He worked at a distributorship that had customers from all over the world. He said the abductors were asking for a five million dollar ransom. The federal government was involved and that's why the public hasn't heard too much about it. McCall agreed, "Oh probably."

"The government don't say much when big bucks is involved," the man said. McCall finished his beer and moved to the other end of the bar to talk to some of his biking buddies. Everyone at this end of the bar was discussing hockey and the bartender didn't serve him because he probably thought he was going to go back to his original seat. He left The Air-Port.

McCall went to another bar where he started talking about the five million bucks to watch the expression on people's faces, hoping to get some reaction. His story must have been the best one because no one could top it. Using this rumour hadn't worked the way he had hoped, he thought to himself.

The conversation here started up on hockey too, so he left this bar as well. He had had two beer. Didn't feel like any more and headed home. He was thinking of Lorraine. He stopped at the corner all night drug store to buy some sleeping pills. He parked his car and went up to his apartment. He suddenly remembered his interview on TV. The chief said it would be on with the ten o'clock news. Perhaps he meant the eleven o'clock news. Anyway, he had missed it. It was now 11:28. He turned on the TV and surprised, saw himself telling his story. The network only showed a short segment of the interview, just enough to keep everyone curious and watching.

As he was pondering another sleepless night, he glanced at his phone. Lo and behold the red light was blinking. He picked it up gingerly, as if it was connected to a bomb and pushed the replay button. He almost fainted. It was Lorraine who had left him an abrupt message saying that she'd be at his place on Sunday afternoon.

"I knew it," he said out loud. Finally he would have a good night's sleep, he thought to himself. He was relieved an considered calling the chief and letting him know Lorraine was okay, but changed his mind. The chief had had enough excitement for the day already. They all had. Besides, why should the chief be concerned about his girlfriend... He turned off the TV and began to undress.

He was about to take a sleeping pill when the phone rang.

"What the hell," he said, as he picked up the receiver.

It was the chief. Stewart was telling him that there was a riot in front of the station. A dozen reporters were demanding to know what was happening with the "Mystery Bus" case. Everyone wants to know what the hell is going on. A US commissioner had called from his office, and he too wanted to know what was going on.

"You had better come in McCall, I can't take this anymore. I am hoarse from talking."

McCall could already hear himself saying, "But chief, I didn't sleep at all last night."

But he didn't say that, instead he said, "I'll be right there." That's what Adams would have said.

Just for curiosity sake he turned the TV on again and switched to CNN. Anderson was reporting on the 'To Hell and Back' case. Journalists seemed to like that description better than the 'Mystery Bus,' which was too bland. Anderson said there were tens of thousands of reporters across the world preoccupied with this kidnapping. This Canadian thing was by far the most newsworthy and the most unusual case ever. Everyone was going nuts, trying to figure it out.

He'd heard enough and put his civilian clothes back on. He went downstairs straight to the drugstore and asked the druggist for something to keep him awake. The druggist asked him if he was alright. McCall asked why.

"You were here a half an hour ago and bought some sleeping pills, now you want some uppers? What is it you want to do? You want to be half asleep?"

The druggist was right. He was confused. He didn't have his uniform on. He was in street clothes.

He told the druggist he had to go back to work and that he was a cop and pulled out his badge to prove it. The druggist felt sorry for him. McCall felt sorry for himself. He wanted to go to his office like the Pope wanted to go to a nudist convention. All he'd heard is a lot of questions that he wouldn't have any answer for. He forced himself into his car and drove slowly. So slowly, that an old lady gave him the one finger salute. Since she didn't know who he was, he returned the gesture.

When he arrived at his office he had no place to park. Every parking place was taken, including his spot, even though it had a 'SUPERINTENDENT' sign on it.

He stopped in the middle of the road and started to raise hell with the reporters. One of them asked him who the hell he thought he was. Again, he pulled out his badge to prove his identity. At this rate he would have it worn out within a week, he figured. In any case it was a bad thing to do. The minute they realized who he was they engulfed him like a tsunami and drowned him in questions. First he wanted to joke with them, but that didn't work. Then he become serious and then they didn't believe him. Then he asked them if they knew anything. Then they started joking. So, all in all, his coming in to the station accomplished absolutely nothing. He told the reporters to go home and unlike himself, get a good night's sleep. Just like good little boys, they listened, and did what he told them to do. Even the reporter who had taken his parking spot left. Now he could park in his own spot.

He went inside. The sergeant was wiping his brow and thanked McCall for rescuing him. McCall said, "No problem," and went into his office.

He wanted to speak with the chief, but his phone was busy.

To pass the time he started thinking about Lorraine again and of all the things they had planned to do before this abduction thing came up. He had to deal with this so she would just have to do something to keep herself entertained until it blew over.

He tried the chief again at five to twelve and he answered.

"Did you wear out your phone yet, chief?" McCall asked sarcastically.

"Wish I didn't have one" the chief replied in a long-suffering tone. He must have been suffering because he couldn't smoke in the house and he too didn't have a clue to the million dollar question.

McCall told him he had dealt with the press and was going to try to get some sleep tonight. The chief said he was going to take his phone off the hook. McCall knew he was just kidding, because that was something he wasn't supposed to do.

As he was leaving the station, the night sergeant asked if he could call him should the press start up again. McCall told him he'd kill him if he called either the chief or himself.

After he parked his car in the garage, he had to walk in front the drugstore again. The druggist was just coming back with a coffee and doughnut. He asked McCall if he was sleepwalking. McCall almost let him have it. The druggist told him he would let him have his 'coffee and doughnut.' McCall gave the druggist a long stern look, said no thanks and went upstairs.

CHAPTER 12

When Lorraine awoke Saturday morning, she opened one eye suspiciously studying a strange pattern of sunlight on the wall. Realizing that she was not at home, she opened her other eye. She knew where she was now. She stuck her hand under the pillow and folded it up into her face. She held it there for a few seconds then kicking off the blankets, she yawned and got up. Only the soft buzzing noise of the bar fridge and the muffled sounds of people frolicking in the pool, broke the silence in the room. She stretched lazily and peered outside through a narrow gap in the curtains. It was a beautiful sunny day. She planned to go swimming right after breakfast.

She got dressed and headed towards the dining room. Besides the two dancers, there were only a few other people occupying separate tables in the dining room. She sat down close to the podium. A waiter came immediately and took her order while pouring her a cup of freshly brewed coffee. The coffee tasted as good as Timmy's if not better. She was debating about the coffee to herself when Date showed up in a new patterned shirt and red shorts. She was pleased to see him.

"So, how did you sleep?" Date asked, with a wide grin on his face.

"Like a log. Everything is too good, simply unbelievable,

don't you agree, Mr Date?" Lorraine said.

"I keep pinching myself... may I join you?" Date asked.

"Oh, certainly. I need a reality check myself. " Lorraine said, pointing to a chair across from her.

"So did you make any money last night?" Date asked.

"I sure did. I am tickled pink, I made a hundred and seventy dollars. How did you do, Mr. Date?"

"I was up to three hundred but dropped down to two twenty when I decided to stop. This money will surely come in handy. I can help my daughter-in-law out now. She will be very happy. What are you going to do with all that money if you don't mind me asking?"

"It's not a whole lot of money but I'll probably put it in the bank. I certainly won't keep it under my pillow. Besides, remember I explained to you about Chance and that we plan to get married – someday; and I'll put that money towards the wedding. He hasn't given me a ring yet. He keeps repeating that stupid saying over and over 'They haven't found a big enough diamond yet'. Actually, I'm getting a little tired of hearing that all the time. Maybe I'll buy one for myself and pretend I'm married."

Date swallowed nervously and said laughing, "Hey, I guess you could buy quite a big one with twenty five thousand dollars."

"It's pretty hard to fake a wedding ring though. Unless I wanted to marry Parker," Lorraine joked.

"Why not?" He looks as if he's single. Would you invite me to the wedding?"

"Sure. You could entertain my mom. Dad passed away last year. Cancer."

"Sorry to hear that," Date said as the waiter arrived with Lorraine's breakfast and Date's coffee. Date said he'd already eaten breakfast and just wanted some more coffee. The two dancers got up from their table and left. Date and Lorraine watched them leave and neither one of them said anything.

"So really, what it do you think about Parker, Mr. Date?"

"He's got to be awfully rich. He's certainly flamboyant.

Are you going to be his bank manager?"

"If he offers me the job, yes."

"How about you, Mr. Date. Are you going to work for Parker?"

"Why not? I'd like to check out what kind of jobs are available. I think I'd have it made here."

"I hope he'll use my bank. I'd have do to some training in the resort business which is, of course no problem. I've been with the RCBC bank for over ten years and I think I know what's going on and I imagine working here would be a fun job."

"He seems to like you. Have you met him before?" Date asked.

"He does appear familiar. I might have met him through some banking business I don't remember. In any case it's good to know a person like Parker. I just hope he realizes I have a boyfriend," Lorraine said, chuckling and continued, "Are you going to do any more gambling, Mr. Date?"

"Oh I don't know. I did want to do a little swimming since it's such a nice day. Are you dressing up for the party tonight? You are going, aren't you?" Date asked.

"I'll be there with bells on. I packed lots of dresses and I think I know which one I'm going to wear. They've arranged to have the Bay Street Boogie Boys. I've heard them play before. They're something else. Do you dance, Mr. Date?"

"I used to oh, ah, about forty years ago. Maybe you could have a dance with Mr. Parker. I'll just watch. I'll be your chaperone. Anyway, don't want to hold you up any longer. I'll see you later Ms. Wilkinson. I'm going to look around a little and then put on my bathing suit and enjoy this beautiful day by the pool."

"See you later, Mr. Date," Lorraine said as she proceeded with her breakfast. She drank her coffee and headed back to her room. She was in room number 29. Date was in room 30.

CHAPTER 13

Parker had had a restless night. He woke up early on
Saturday morning and that strange feeling was coming
back. It was that strange feeling that had rippled through
his body when he had touched Lorraine's hand at the poker table.
Was it because he was an adult now? He hadn't counted on
feelings like this. This wasn't part of his plan. He would just have
to deal with it, he thought to himself. She certainly was a bright
business person with a wonderful personality. What did she think
of him? She probably thought of him like an employee might
think of an employer. What would happen if he revealed his
identity? He couldn't do that!

  What now? She had a boyfriend. They both had money.
Were they engaged? She wasn't wearing a ring. Does she love
him? Does he love her? Parker was full of questions about
Lorraine and Chance. They must have been seeing each other for
years - three, four, maybe even five years. What was Chance
waiting for? If he wanted to marry her why didn't he? They
weren't even living together. Maybe McCall is just stringing her
along. Parker began to think he should just hang back to wait and
see if anything developed between them. But what was this? He
wasn't looking for a lover or a wife! He was just looking for his
'mommy'.

  He wanted to lock everything out of his mind except

Lorraine. He dozed off.

In his dream, then he was downstairs in front of a band, entering a dance contest with Lorraine. They started in the middle of the dance floor moving to a fast rhythm, twisting, going down to the floor, standing up. All the passengers got up from the tables and surrounded them. Lorraine's moves were full of lust. He had yellow shorts on, and Lorraine was wearing a white blouse and a red mini skirt and thongs instead of panties. The music was getting louder and louder. He had never danced like this before. She started bumping her hip onto his, and now she was undoing her blouse and unhooking her bra. Her large breasts were bouncing up and down. Sweat was glistening on her body. She broke away from him while everyone was clapping to the sound of wild rock and roll. He was jerking and thrusting as he tried to mimic her. She was calling to him to come and hold her hand and he did. He tore off his shirt and saw himself with a masculine body twisting and twirling. Lorraine stepped out of her skirt and began gyrating in her thongs. The passengers were roaring, giving her more and more room. One of the musicians with a saxophone came down onto the dance floor and started playing a wild beat just for her. She clutched him around his waist with her legs and now he was swinging her out and picking her up, all the while the screaming crowd was egging them on.
He grabbed her hand and began twirling her around, plunging her to the floor and stepping over her. The ecstatic crowd was wailing to the beat now. He started dancing away from her doing the splits, and while he was on his knees, she began shimmying up to him thrusting her belly out seductively. He kissed her below her navel and threw her to the floor. Amid wild screams and hoots and hollers he grabbed her by her honey blonde hair and gave her a long and passionate kiss. Everyone started applauding and thunderously thumping their feet on the floor... they both got up and took a bow. Date came onto the floor and presented him with the highest honor a silver cup.

With a jolt he woke up, perspiring profusely. Grasping his

116

penis, he rolled out of bed and staggered to his shower and turned on all the jets.

Lorraine wasn't blonde. It had to be someone else! He stood under the shower spray with legs that felt like rubber and kept repeating; it couldn't have been her, it wasn't me either, it was not meeeeee! He stayed in the shower for ten to fifteen minutes, wrapped himself in a large towel and sat back down on his bed.

It was seven o'clock. The bedding was all wet from his sweat. Staring at himself in the closet mirror, he saw a wild man with hair sticking out in every direction. He was shivering. The air conditioning must have been set too low, he thought. However, it was always kept at 25C.

He saw dark blotches on his face. There were black circles under his eyes and some of his pimples had started to show again.

How can a person who has never slept with a woman dream of something so wild and lewd? This was another first. He was confused, disoriented and suffering through flashes of perverted thoughts. He combed his hair, brushed his teeth and dabbed some medicated cream onto the visible red spots on his face. He got dressed in a lavender polo shirt and cream coloured pants. White socks and shoes completed his attire. He sprayed on some Gucci cologne which made him smell pleasant. He took the elevator down from his penthouse to the dining room hoping he'd feel better once he had something to eat.

A waiter arrived and looked at him curiously. Parker appeared to be suffering. He must have had a rough night, the waiter thought.

"I'll have eggs Benedict and coffee. That's all, John. How are you?"

The waiter replied that he was fine and that he would be even better later this afternoon when his shift was over. Parker grinned at him and asked for the morning paper. He read all the outrageous commentaries about the abduction and smiled coyly. His smile however, hardened quickly into the look of a determined, goal oriented businessman.

Visions of the dream with the blonde woman began to haunt him. This nightmare seemed so real.

While eating his breakfast, he was pondering over his future conduct with Lorraine.

~

At eight thirty he had a meeting with the security/grounds manager, Max Phillips and his business manager Dallas Matheson. He informed them that Lorraine was going to be the future bank manager. They were happy to hear that, as they found her very pleasant. He then asked if anyone had any concerns. They had none. Obviously no one had noticed the two women walking to the road to buy drugs last night.

Matheson had all the expenses for this event at the resort documented and had made a forecast for the remaining bills. The photographers were arriving at 10am and they would be taking pictures all day and into the evening. Expenditures to date were $830,000 plus $3,000 paid out so far for casino winnings, and $18,000 paid out for the stores. Even with the photographer's bill and the limousines tomorrow, the total cost would still be well below the budgeted 1.2 million. The lawyer and additional bills from the railroad, RCMP, and local police were on a different budget.

"Oh, I almost forgot," said Mattison, "I got a hold of the magician Lucas Wilson from Port Dover and he will be here at seven for the dinner entertainment."

"Super," Parker replied with thoughts of wishing there was a magical way to figure out the meaning of his weird dream.

The money didn't bother Parker. Lorraine did. He had barely heard Matheson talking as his mind was preoccupied with screwed up sexual feelings. He couldn't decide whether to approach Lorraine this morning or just wait. He knew he would have to do something soon. Perhaps he should just leave things up in the air, and see what happens.

Turning to his two managers he said, "I am going to plan the final chapter in what they call the 'Mystery Bus' case. I like that description. I wonder who came up with that name. I'll have everything ready for you at two o'clock this afternoon."

CHAPTER 14

After breakfast, Lorraine went to her room and put on the yellow bikini that she had packed. It was three years old but it still fit. She liked it because the top was comfortable. She was happy that she had not gained any weight.

She turned on the TV and the local weather report showed nothing but sunshine for the coming three days. The announcer said the temperature was 27 and was going up to 32 in the afternoon. She couldn't have asked for a better day. There were more than a dozen people in the pool already, some diving, some swimming and others playing with a ball. Lorraine was a strong swimmer and would do six laps just to get her system going.

As she was climbing out of the pool a flock of camera people encircled her and started snapping pictures. She didn't mind but she would have appreciated a little time to comb her hair at least, she said. Some photographers laughed and said her hair was perfect. Nevertheless they summoned the makeup crew who did a magnificent job on her hair almost instantaneously. She was beginning to like all the attention she was getting.

The crew brought out an assortment of sunglasses and she tried them all on and chose the ones she liked best. She had good taste in glasses, the ones she chose were designer glasses, priced at $349.99. She got them cheap. Free, of course. They brought different bathing suits for her as well, but still she liked her own the best. The picture taking went on for more than three quarters of an hour and she was getting tired of posing.

"Just a few more... just a couple more shots," the photographers cried.

~

From his penthouse window Parker was watching the action below. All the while being tormented by the dream he had last night. His body was going through major changes for sure. Changes he didn't understand. He had a few drinks to help him think, and the alcohol told him to stay away from Lorraine as much as possible. Let things take their natural course! He took the alcohol's advice. He moved away from the window and turned on the TV.

~

Once the photographers were done with Lorraine, she laid down on a lounge chair and started thinking about McCall. He also liked sun tanning and was a strong swimmer too. She was thinking about the good times they had spent together on some remote islands snorkeling and diving. But she felt increasingly bitter now, especially being alone and the centre of attention.

She got the suntan lotion from her beach bag and sprayed her arms and legs and as much of her back as she could reach. Seeing her predicament, a young man from the makeup crew came over and offered to do her back.

As he was about to start some small talk, he was called away to do another 'spraying' job on the two dancers. They were livelier and far more provocative than Lorraine. And they opted for rather flimsy beach wear as well. They had more audience too. All the young guys were more than eager to be in pictures with them.

Date moseyed up behind Lorraine, sporting a beer belly, but upon seeing her reading a magazine he simply walked by without saying anything. But he couldn't help admiring her curvaceous body.

~

As noon approached, someone turned on the music and two of the Hungarian chefs began to set up the barbecue. The bar opened as well. Lorraine got a hamburger and went back to her lounger chair. Seeing her unaccompanied, Date got a couple drinks, one for Lorraine and one for himself.

"What more could one ask for...?" he said to Lorraine as he offered her the drink while praising the luxury and the abundance of beverages at the bar.

"Oh, how nice of you, Mr. Date. I was just thinking of a refreshment myself. Thank you very much," she said, sitting up. Date pulled over one of the lounger chairs and set it up in the shade beside her.

"They must have taken a thousand pictures of you, Ms. Wilkinson. Hope you get some copies of them for yourself. Have you ever thought of modelling?"

"Yes I have, for about two seconds. I'd have to be at least three sizes smaller for starters. I am too fat, Mr. Date."

Date didn't want to argue. She looked like a model to him. She looked absolutely gorgeous. His attention was captured by the two dancers who were having a ball. They were moving to the fast beat of the music. They were wishing secretly that they had a brass pole to dance with and nothing on. Judging by the looks on their faces, so did the men around them. Considering their lewd movements, Date got to thinking they were strippers or something along that line and he mentioned this to Lorraine. She agreed. And of course that's what they were, though no one knew.

Now that the bar was open, the younger chaps were starting to feel pretty happy. Sounds of laughter and hooting came from the pool and every time someone did a cannonball the water splashed everywhere. One of the passengers, Tia Sinclair brought out her guitar and started singing. An outdoor microphone was already set up. She sang beautifully. Everyone asked who she was. Of course she was simply Tia Sinclair, the 'unknown'. She was visibly very pleased. With the twenty-five thousand and perhaps with some help from Parker, she hoped things would soon change. And she was in luck. Parker had just arrived, liked what he had heard and asked her to sit down with him to discuss a job at the resort. Perhaps a different woman would get his mind off his alarming dream. He planned to find out.

Lorraine noticed the two and wondered what they were talking about. They certainly wouldn't be talking about banking business, she thought. She watched Parker getting a hotdog and stopping to talk to a young man - Imre Varga, the student from Budapest who didn't speak good English. Everyone had gotten to know him at last night's dinner where the Hungarian chefs had introduced him. While he spoke very little English, he understood enough to take Parker's advice about learning the language and staying in Canada to finish his schooling. Parker would sponsor him. The young student had particularly impressed Parker when he announced that his plan was to major in computer electronics.

Imre was happier than he had ever been. It was the opportunity of a lifetime. This would certainly be a big help to his parents who were struggling to pay for his tuition back in the old country. In his broken English he exclaimed, "tank yu, tank yu. Mr. Parker."

After a 'couple' of drinks the two dancers got a craving for some 'weed' but they also relished the attention at the pool. Luckily, the photographers had broken for lunch giving the girls a chance to go back to Lisa's room for a smoke. They immediately bombed out and slept for two hours, missing the hotdogs, the hamburgers, the drinks – everything at the poolside barbecue. Lorraine decided to leave too. She left Date and went to her room for a rest.

~

Phillips and Matheson arrived at Parker's penthouse at two

o'clock sharp and got down to business right away.

"This is the plan," Parker began, "Tomorrow after all the passengers have been taken home, one of you will call our friend Chance McCall. Who wants the job?"

He spoke in tones that would have charmed a ninety year old grandmother into robbing a bank.

"I'll do it," Phillips said laughing, "and will likely spend the rest of my life in jail."

"We will miss you," Parker replied with a sombre look on his face. "Seriously, once everyone, and I mean everyone, is back home, one of the limousine drivers will contact you. You then get hold of McCall. He should be in his office. Tell him we were the ones who rented the 'Mystery Bus'. Identify yourself and tell him all the passengers are safely back home. This will shock him. He won't understand what's going on. He'll probably give you a hassle but he'll be too befuddled to come to any conclusions. He will likely want to talk to you in person right away. Either he will come to meet with you here or he will want you to go to the police station.

Once you've talked to him, call me and I'll put Lorraine in a limo and send her to McCall's apartment. This will likely be in the afternoon. By that time McCall will have spoken with Chief Stewart and told him the 'awesome' news. The two will undoubtedly get together to prepare a statement for the press. They will not know exactly what to report and they will want to talk to me. Tell them I am not available. Tell them you represent the company and they can only talk to you. Tell them we did this fake abduction purely as a publicity stunt. Tell them everyone will be compensated for their trouble, including the police. They will not believe you at first but then you show them the blank cheque, which I'll give you right now.

You are not to go into any details about the passengers and if they get tough call our lawyer Drew Bundy and he'll take over. He knows what's going on. I'll be in touch with him.

You see, if no one complains - there's no case."

"What about WRL?" Phillips asked.

"They'll be compensated as well," Parker said and continued, "the key person is Lorraine. I'll make certain she doesn't say anything derogatory, which of course she won't because she's going to be our bank manager. She will talk about the good time everyone had and all the free stuff she and everybody received. You emphasize to McCall the good times. You must follow my instructions to the letter and in the order that I have given you. If you get stuck, call me. I'm giving you a printout so that you can memorize everything."

"Now, once McCall has spoken to Lorraine and has found out that she is going to be our bank manager, he will support her. You see... he will be on our side. He will become our ally. Whatever he and Stewart release to the newspapers will be positive, or at least neutral. That is a guarantee. Everyone likes money. Money corrupts people. Money corrupts politicians, governments, everybody. The difference in this case is that it is my own money and it comes from me! Not from the people, not from taxes. I earned this money honestly. Do you understand?"

"Got you," Phillips said.

"Just watch how this story will ripple throughout the whole world. I am dying to see what the international press will say about this. It's getting exciting now, eh? Any questions?"

"What if they start getting tough?" Phillips asked.

"You call Bundy, right away. If you can't find him, call me. They won't get tough. Remember there are no victims. For the time being, you guys enjoy yourselves. That's an order. Tomorrow will be a busy day." Parker said. As the two left his room, Parker sidestepped his robotic bartender, reached into the ice bucket and made himself a drink of white rum and soda water manually.

~

After a good rest Lorraine went to the pool one more time and did a few more laps. The photographers took a few more pictures of her then set her free, stating that was all the water shots they wanted of her. As she sat back on her lounge chair, she took another glance up at the building and noticed Parker standing in one of the windows looking down at her. She didn't think much of it. He could have been looking at just about anybody. He might have been looking at the hair dressers, or Tia Sinclair or anyone. Surely, he wasn't just watching her. He didn't have to. Especially if she was going to be working for him. Nonetheless it was strange that she saw him at the window... He could simply have come down again... She dismissed these thoughts.

As a matter of fact, Parker was looking at Lorraine and feeling pressure in his groin. His mind was racing back and forth from his school years and all the years he had been missing her. Finally she was here. And she will now be around him all the time. How was he going to interact with her now? He wanted to be with her all the time, but he knew that was impossible. No one can be with someone all the time.

He poured himself another stiff rum on ice and drank it down in two gulps. The warm feeling inside him got even warmer. However the tightness in his groin eased only momentarily. He pulled a chair up to the window and secretively watched Lorraine combing her hair and spraying lotion on her body. He saw another man arrive to spray lotion on her. He had an almost uncontrollable urge to go down and shove the young man aside and take over, assist her, maybe... just start talking to her.

But if he did go down, what would he say to her? Was he going to talk to her about his dream of last night? Was he going to apologize to her about his dream or was he going to tell her that it was just a dream and laugh about it. He was not even a good dancer, and he certainly didn't have the body he had in his dream.

What about kissing her on her belly? He couldn't talk about that for sure. He realized that his conversational skills with women were sorely lacking. In the past, when he spoke with females it was all business. What do men say to women? He realized now he wasn't thinking of Lorraine as he used to, his

126

'mommy' now had become a sex object.

Would she help him if he confessed and told her he'd never slept with a woman before? Would she take that as a virtue or would she take that as a weakness or would she laugh at him? Would she humiliate him? Ridicule him? Or would she deny him? Would she report him for sexual harassment? Could this be called a form of terrorism of the mind? What if he gave her money. Could she be bought for money? Everything was becoming sexual. Everything was sexual. This whole abduction could be twisted into a sex scandal. It was all designed around her and the players - his employees - were just pawns forced to go along with him.

He wasn't a heavy drinker and for that reason the booze went to his head fast. And now he had to have another drink. That one went to his legs. He laid down in his bed. He had never been inebriated before. This was another new road he was going down.

He started to get frightened. Sex scandal... What will the shareholders think of a sex scandal at the Eagle Hills Resort? Suicide? Too much.. too much to bear.... Have to end it right now... while it can still be ended. But how?

Panic stricken, he got up and went to his vault and opened it. He remembered a special potion he had gotten from a native healer, a Medicine Man who told him to use it as a last resort, only when everything seemed lost and there was no way out. This will give him unbelievable power, and open up never before imagined insight. But he failed to remember that he was not to take any of this potion alone. Someone had to be with him when he took it, just to be sure he didn't take too much. He found the tiny packet and opened it. He stared at the white substance a second or two and emptied most of it into a glass of water and drank it. Almost instantly total delirium took over.

CHAPTER 15

Parker became a crazed man and a crazed man cannot reason. Parker felt cornered, threatened, and his bizarre imagination began to run wild. In this daze he envisioned the police coming after him. His mind imagined McCall finding Lorraine in a bed lying on her back in her yellow bikini all tied up with tape across her mouth. There were others in rooms, tied to bed posts and taped. Through his mental fog, he saw all the doors to the rooms wide open. McCall had arrived to take Lorraine away, to rescue her.

"I won't let her go! She's staying here!" Parker shouted aloud in his delirium. In his crazed mind, he was outside now defending the 'cabin' behind the barbed-wire fence. In his haze he found himself at Armstrong's cabin with his classmates and his 'mommy'. They were all there to help him out with his explosives. He was ready for a battle.

In his stupor, Parker began giving orders, "Put three grenades at the gate, two at every post, a dozen around the cabin and one in the outhouse. Booby trap the water pump and put twenty grenades around the pond. Put the rocket launcher in the middle of the soccer field. Mannen... where is Mannen? Open the rear gate and let the bears in. Oh wait... the bears are already in? Yes, I can see them now. Get the hunters. They are on our side.

We have to keep this cabin open. The cabin is our command centre. Come sit by the fire, sing with us...or, ok fine, I don't care. Catch your fish first. We'll fry the fish. They taste good. I raised them from goldfish. See how big they are? Hurry! Double up the barbed wire fence!! Got to keep the police out! Is that a helicopter? Are they attacking? I see the tribal chief, wearing his war bonnet. He's with us too. Hello, Mr. Tribal Chief. What have you got for me? Drummers! Drummers? Drum louder, louder! Oh God, the police are here. What? They're on horseback. Oh, mounted police. ...ha ha ha. Come on... give me that knife. Not the broken one. Give me a new knife! I'll get that son of a bitch with that stick. Hit, hit, hit. Hit his bald head, his red bald head. Ahh, I have to pee teacher. Let me out. Let me pee. Hoooleeey, just look at all the blisters on my arm. They don't hurt. They smell a little. Mommy, where are you mommy? Mommy, please comb my hair. Will you, will you, mommy?"

Parker was experiencing excruciating pain and a high fever. The potion wasn't going to let him out easily. Was it because the Medicine Man wasn't there? Or was it because he'd had too much alcohol. He stood up and aimed his head towards the ceiling and screamed. But no one heard him, and the automatic security system didn't care. It wasn't programmed to think, or solve personal problems.

Bewildered, he fell backwards onto his bed and fought with his satin sheets. Perspiration was gushing from his body and he was dehydrating rapidly. His mouth and throat became dry and his vision blurred. He fell off his bed and began to crawl on the floor. When he got close to the wall he tried to climb it. His fingers sank into the wallcovering, tearing parts of it away. He was crawling around aimlessly and by accident he hit a button that switched on the automatic bartender on the bar. The machine was confused because it hadn't been given any further command. While trying to get up he clumsily palmed the button again and the automate took this as a command for whiskey. It sprayed whiskey into his face. Parker gagged and shook his head. In a

129

murky frame of mind, he poked around for shut off controls. But he again hit the wrong buttons and the machine squirted coke onto his pants instead. Wet now from head to toe he slid on the expensive drenched carpet and hit his head on the coffee table. Trying to get up, he fell backwards and hit his head heavily on the bar. He dropped to his knees and flattened out on his stomach. However the worst was yet to come. In his frenzy, rolling his eyes wildly, he staggered to his feet. He poked at thin air and started fighting an imagined ghost that appeared before him. With an uppercut, he hit himself squarely on the chin. This almost knocked him out. Somehow, he staggered into the bathroom as he fought off three zombies and twisted their heads into pretzels. Pretzels which were actually the shower handles. Water started to gush with seemingly the same power as Niagara Falls and with about the same volume. If he was wet before, he was now thoroughly soaked. His lavender shirt and his cream coloured pants looked like camouflage now and the pimples on his face had morphed into crimson red potholes, resembling large ladybugs.

To escape the gushing shower, his crazed mind directed him towards the Jacuzzi where he fumbled around with some more knobs and buttons. Unaware of what he was doing, he accidentally turned on the cold water then the hot and started splashing around. He groped around and hit more buttons and had water streaming from all directions. Sweet aroma filled the room and a symphony began playing gently from the ceiling speakers. The music enveloped the bathroom and were it not for the noise of the small river flowing down the drain, it would have been quite enjoyable. This entire journey all happened over the span of three minutes. And things kept happening. The shower drain got plugged with towels, and water began flowing out into the living room, and out under the door into the elevator shaft, where it shorted out the circuits.

An alarm sounded. Phillips came running and turned off the water. He was shocked and confused himself and called for an ambulance. Parker was taken to the hospital. A doctor examined him right away but other than for being drunk, he could not diagnose him with anything. However, Phillips approached the doctor with a small plastic pouch which he had found on the floor of Parker's room and gave it to the doctor. It was discovered by the lab to be Sacred Datura and the doctor knew right away that this had been the cause of Parker's delirium, hallucinations, delusions and stupor.

"Let's hope he didn't take it with vodka," the doctor commented to Phillips.

"Why, Doc?" Phillips asked.

"Vodka is made with grain germs, and the combination could create a health problem down the road. Datura and grain germs don't mix," the doctor said. He began injecting an antidote into Parker's IV bag. The drug put Parker to sleep instantly.

~

Lorraine felt she had had enough sun. Her back started to burn and there was a distinct white line under her watch band. She thought she might as well go to her room and try on some of the dresses she had brought with her. They just didn't look right though when she put them on. They were wrinkled and she had no iron. What the heck, let's see if I can find one I like in the STORES, she thought.

After spending some time in the well stocked ladies department, she found a gorgeous emerald-green silk dress for $780.00 plus tax. She thought the price was a little high but decided to try it on anyway. The dress fit her perfectly. The sales lady rang in the price with the tax, and her bill came to zero. It was hard to believe, but it was indeed on the house, and that made the shopping exhilarating. She went back to her room and put it on again. It fit magnificently and it accentuated all her vital curves. All she needed was a diamond necklace. She laughed. Maybe Parker would buy her one if she asked. But then she thought, who was she kidding other than herself. Little did she know Parker would have bought her anything she asked for. She had no idea about Parker's present predicament.

Since she had not planned on a dress up event, she had brought no jewellery with her and her pretty dress wouldn't look right without jewellery. She didn't think Parker would mind if she went to the STORES and bought a simple little necklace. She took off her new dress and put the old one back on. She had lots of time. It was only ten after four. She went to the STORES again and to her great surprise the store was full of female passengers, all of them shopping. Everyone suddenly realized that shopping in this store would be fun and exciting. They could buy anything they wanted for zero dollars. Wasn't this every woman's dream? She looked for the longest time for something nice that would go with her dress. Finally she decided on an imitation emerald-zirconium necklace, retail price $1,389.99. The cashier rang in the item, again it came to zero dollars. Lorraine was beginning to enjoy this kind of shopping. Under her breath and mischievously she said, "Eat your heart out, Mr. Parker."

Then she thought, without a bracelet and matching ring, she would feel naked. Can't have that! She forced herself back to the jewellery department and laboriously searched until she found the bracelet and ring she needed. This time the total came to $1,287.60 with tax. Her price however, once more came to zero dollars. She was having the time of her life.

She suddenly realized how easy it was to blow thirty-five hundred dollars. She was glad it wasn't her own money. Trying to contain her excitement, she hurried back to her room.

She tried her dress on again, along with the jewellery and felt like a celebrity. She looked it too. She had to hand it to Parker. He really knew how to spoil his prospective employees.

Oh, oh, shoes... have to find the right shoes for this dress. Can't go to a dance in sandals! Everybody knows that, she thought. Back to STORES she went, and half an hour later she left with an elegant pair priced at $489.90. That was expensive, even for the rich. When the clerk rang in the price and gave her the tab, she didn't even look at it. She knew it was correct.

If Lorraine thought her shopping for free was extravagant,

she should have seen the two 'movie stars'. They looked grotesque with the things they bought. They of course lacked sophistication.

She went and had her hair done. Then it was time to get ready. All she needed was McCall but she knew he couldn't be there. She wanted to cry, but that would have spoiled her mascara. Actually, this was the very first time she was without him. And in light of that this was the first time she had a chance to think about their relationship.

She could see that he wasn't keen on tying the knot. She could see he liked things just the way they were. Every once in a while when they got together for a week or two to play house, seemed to be enough for him. During these times they got along great. He concentrated on doing things with her rather than going out to play cards or drinking with his buddies. It was clear to her that if they were to get married, it would change his bachelor-style life which he probably would not want to give up. McCall wasn't a mind reader. Had he been aware of how she felt, he would have insisted they talk it over. Lorraine decided not to think about their relationship anymore this evening, as she wanted to enjoy herself.

Making all those purchases that cost her no money, put her in a very good mood. As she was leaving her room, she almost knocked Date over. He was looking debonair and smelling like a perfume factory.

"Mr. Date, you are dressed to kill. Are you going to a wedding?" she asked the startled man.

"I thought you were going to mow me down," Date said. He hadn't been watching where he was going because he had his mind on something else.

"Well, I don't even know how to begin to tell you. I've met this lady, Anita Todd, and it was love at first sight. She is a divorcee with a grown-up daughter and also has a business. She's on a business trip now."

"Fantastic. Good for you Mr. Date!"

"You look absolutely smashing, Ms. Wilkinson. Let's sit together, if you don't mind?"

"Definitely not," Lorraine said feeling really happy for Date.

"Catch you later then," Date said excusing himself as he rushed off to get Anita from room 26.

Isn't that great, Lorraine thought. Everybody loves somebody, sometime. She wondered where she had heard that phrase before.

~

In the dining room, Lorraine chose a table in the last row from the stage and took a seat facing the activity. The dance floor was between the stage and the tables. There were some people setting up equipment and instruments and a projection screen as if they were getting ready to show a movie.

To her great surprise she saw Lucas Wilson and Missy on the stage preparing to do a show.

They couldn't see her because the dining room was dimly lit. She thought maybe she would send a message to McCall. But she decided not to. In fact, she didn't even want them to notice her. If they were going to put on a show, she just wanted to enjoy it.

She saw Date and Anita coming in and she waved them over. Anita Todd needed no introduction since Lorraine had previously met her at the STORES.

"I guess it's just going to be the three of us unless I can send a taxi for Chance," Lorraine said ruefully.

"That's a bummer," said Anita as she sat down on the chair Date was holding out for her.

Noticing the awkward positioning of the chairs around the table, Lorraine moved to the right thus allowing Anita to sit beside her facing the stage.

The photographers invaded the room and started taking

pictures of everyone. Some prizes had been drawn and awarded to a few lucky people. Not wanting to waste any time, Wilson introduced himself and his 'stagehand' Missy and started telling jokes. Everyone howled. Then he did some magic tricks and made Missy disappear. When she reappeared, she was walking back towards the stage from the rear of the dining room. During the performance, waiters were busy setting up for dinner. Every time a waiter went in or out of the kitchen the aroma of mouth-watering roast beef flooded the dining room.

Wilson asked one of the dancers, Karen, up on stage. He asked her to spread out a deck of cards face up on the table in four rows of thirteen cards per row. Just before she did that, he asked Missy to blindfold him.

When Karen was finished, Wilson asked Missy to project the cards onto the screen and then asked her to take off his blindfold and let him look at them.

He looked at the cards for a few seconds. Turning away from the screen he called out the random cards one after the other not making a single mistake. Everyone was amazed except Lorraine, but she didn't let on. Wilson stated that he could remember tens of thousands of cards randomly because he had a photographic memory. Lorraine knew that too and wished she had that talent. Maybe then she could remember where she had seen Parker before.

When the magic show ended, the Wilsons left and dinner was served. The musicians took over the stage and started setting up and tuning their instruments. Strangely, Parker was nowhere to be seen. Lorraine thought he would have been one of the first ones here.

"Don't you think it's unusual that Parker's not here, Mr. Date?"

"It is strange indeed. Maybe he's with his people at the back of the dining room." But of course he wasn't. He was just about waking up in the hospital.

The roast beef dinner, salads and dessert were another culinary masterpiece. The Hungarian chefs received another standing ovation.

~

"Testing, one-two-three, one-two-three," came from a set of high powered speakers.

"Well, we've got about an hour to kill before the dance starts, it's only eight o'clock. Let's go make some money in the casino," Date suggested and got up.

"Not a bad idea," Lorraine replied.

A waiter came and asked if Date wanted to save the table.

Date said "Sure, it's a good spot." The waiter put a 'reserved' sign on the table and left.

"Let's try our luck for the last time," Date said and stepped aside to let the women lead the way to the casino.

As they were leaving, Date wondered aloud about the people at the rear of the dining room. Perhaps they were special guests of Parker's, he exclaimed but never gave it another thought. They had to be guests since they were dressed up, Lorraine thought.

And they were guests. They were guests of Phillips and Matheson and a few mid-management people.

When Lorraine and company returned from the casino the music was already playing. The band played a Rock-a-Billy number that sounded better and louder than the original. A lot of young people were dancing, including the 'beauticians'.

Lorraine would have danced too if she had had someone to dance with. Instead, she just sat tapping her feet to the rhythm.

CHAPTER 16

While hundreds of drug deals go unnoticed, some are outstanding or notable. Barely notable was the deal at the Eagle Hills Resort on Friday night. On Saturday, RCMP Sergeant Guy Dubois reported two known users and their dealer to the police commissioner. He reported seeing them at an unusual location, but Commissioner Marcel Lefebvre didn't get overly excited.

To him it was a simple deal, just another case out of thousands that go on every minute of every day, everywhere. Dubois agreed. The only thing unusual about this deal however, Dubois said, was that the resort wasn't open yet.

"How did you find this out?" Lefebvre asked Dubois.

"We had this dealer, Matthew Sommers under surveillance, and two strippers called him for some drugs last night. The girls said they were at the Eagle Hills Resort. First of all the resort is not open to the public and second, they don't have a permit for dancers. So we tailed Sommers to the resort where he made the deal with the dancers. The deal went off by the side of the road and the women went back to the resort. There is a large area cleared for construction and there's all kinds of equipment around the existing buildings. The strippers went into one of those buildings. The gated entrance was closed, so our man didn't go in to investigate," Dubois said.

"Let's turn this over to the local OPP. They should be able to handle this. Just give them the paperwork and let them do the rest," Lefebvre said. Dubois nodded his head.

~

Eagle Hills Resort was in the jurisdiction of the Greater Toronto Area OPP. By the time the request trickled down to them it was 5pm on Saturday afternoon. And Chief Hudson's office of the GTA OPP, didn't receive the note until 9am Sunday. Since it wasn't an emergency, it was put off until Monday. Besides, what was the hurry, the duty sergeant thought. The resort would be there Sunday, Monday and every day. Just in case there was any more illicit activity happening there, he assigned a couple of cruisers for surveillance of the resort.

"Keep an eye out for the girls too," the sergeant instructed the officers. "They might have some new suppliers muscleing in."

CHAPTER 17

Totally oblivious to what had happened to him, Parker was wondering why he was in the hospital. He vaguely remembered worrying about Lorraine and drinking heavily.

"Look at me, I'm telling people to watch their liquor and here I am waking up with a head as big as a beach ball and a hangover that would cripple a bull.

A nurse came in grinning from ear to ear telling him about the 'little mischief' he'd gotten himself into. Parker didn't know what she was talking about. Not wanting to complicate things, he just shook his head and sucked on his teeth. He asked the nurse for water. The hallucinatory drug Datura had caused a temporary short term memory loss. He wanted to get up, but his legs wouldn't support him. The nurse had to help him sit up at the side of the bed. Phillips entered the room and looked at Parker curiously. Thinking the two wanted privacy, the nurse left the room.

"How are you doing, boss? Phillips asked Parker cautiously.

"I'm fine, except for a gigantic headache. What happened...why am I here in the hospital?"

Charles Eric Jambor

"You had some bad drugs this afternoon, boss."
"Me drugs..."
"Yeah, the doctor says you got into some drugs you had in your vault. He didn't say what it was. You trashed your apartment, but we're getting it straightened up, right now."

Parker ran the back of his hand under his nose, then pinched his ear lobe, trying very hard to recollect. Everything was vague and distant. His mind was navigating in a thick fog with no lighthouse in sight.

"Get me out of here. I want to go home. I've got work to do."

"Just a minute boss, I've got to check on something." Phillips went to the nurse's desk to talk to the doctor. The doctor was there but wasn't going to let Parker go home. But Phillips insisted, "He has a very important function going on Doc, I have to take him home."

"Well, then someone has to keep an eye on him all the time. He's in a trance and he is high. We could bring him down slowly in four to five days or maybe I could give him an antidote injection..." the doctor said with hesitation.

"We'll watch him like a hawk. Please give him the shot right now." After the doctor administered the injection, Phillips and his assistant dressed Parker in fresh clothes. As they were leaving the emergency room the doctor pulled Phillips aside and in a hushed but stern tone said, "No alcohol of any sort. Not even tomorrow or next week. He mustn't have alcohol for at least a couple of months! And he's got to come back here on Monday."
Phillips promised to bring him back himself.

As they were going downstairs to the limousine a very dark idea came into Phillips' mind. What would happen if he blackmailed Parker. He could make a lot of money on this incident. He was certain Parker wouldn't want anyone to know about what happened at his penthouse. He'd get the video recording from the room and make a copy of it. It wouldn't even have to be him who did the blackmailing. He could hire

140

somebody off the street...He could pay the guy out of Parker's money. Phillips knew Parker trusted him. All he had to do was feed him misinformation. Parker was paranoid already. He'd just build on this to scare him more. He could get hundreds of thousands of dollars, maybe even millions out of him. He could tell the police Parker was crazy... they would believe him once he told them what had happened in the penthouse. No. He couldn't do that. Parker was too powerful. Besides he had a good paying job. Why upset the applecart?

They got into the limousine.

By the time Parker arrived back home, his penthouse had been repaired, the carped dried and the wall fixed. The electronics had been checked and reprogrammed where needed.

"Where is Lorraine... Was she up here with me or am I imaging things?" he asked Phillips.

"No, boss. You were all alone. We came running when the alarm went off. We thought you were robbed because your vault was open."

Slowly the fog started to diminish and reality began to settle in. There was an awful taste in his mouth and an emptiness in his stomach. His legs were weak and his arms felt heavy. He asked Phillips for some Alka-Seltzer and food.

"We'll fix you up, boss. I'll get you something to eat. You better lay down and rest." Hurriedly, Phillips went to the kitchen and asked the chef for something to cure a bad hangover. He didn't mention any names. He rushed back just in time to find Parker getting out his makeup and preparing to apply it to his face.

"It's past nine. I want to see my guests. Are they enjoying themselves?"

"They are all right. Everybody's fine, boss."

The door bell rang and the waiter entered with a glass of water and the Alka-Seltzer and a plate of sauerkraut and smoked turkey sausages. The food was recommended by the head Hungarian chef who said it was designed to cure a hangover and an unstable stomach.

"Try it boss. The chef says it will cure you."

Actually the food did work a miracle on Parker, he didn't even have to take the Alka-Seltzer.

"Rest for a while boss, I'll be back in a bit and we'll go downstairs," Phillips said. Before he left the penthouse he turned on the surveillance system to monitor what was happening in Parker's room. The blackmail idea began to reformulate in his mind. He could ask for two million... Parker's got tons of money. But how would he get it? That was the only snag. He would have to work that out... first though, he would have to take everyone home... then he'd only have Parker to deal with.

~

Parker took Phillips' advice and rested in his huge recliner. His mind drifted back to Lorraine. His hangover seemed almost negligible compared to the mixed emotions he still had about her. To get her off his mind, he turned on the TV and watched a news channel. To his great surprise the station showed the ending of an interview with Superintendent McCall. He wished he had seen the whole segment and made a mental note to watch it later on the same channel. The presenter started talking about abductions across the world. Now it's started in Canada too. Parker smiled mischievously. During a commercial he got up from his chair and went into the bathroom to put medicated cream on his face. While dabbing it on, he began to look a little better, but the cream didn't ease the pounding between his temples. That nagging question returned, "What am I going to say to her tonight?" he asked out loud. It's now or never he thought. He had to make a move and find out how she really felt about him. Obviously she hadn't recognized him, so he had to reveal himself to her! But how...?

Phillips came back and the two of them went down to the dining room. It was almost half past nine and the band was playing. Parker searched for Lorraine but he couldn't see her. He panicked. What if she didn't show? That couldn't happen. She had

142

to be here, he thought. He was all nerves as he sat down with his managers and asked the waiter for a coffee.

Tia Sinclair arrived on stage to sing with the band and she distracted him momentarily. At the end of her song Tia waved to him and bowed and he applauded vigorously. When the musicians recessed, he scanned the room for Lorraine again and this time he noticed her sitting with Date away from the bandstand. In his mind he practised different ways to approach her.

Having arrived from the casino just a few minutes after Parker sat down, Lorraine and company were discussing their luck at the blackjack table. Without asking, a waiter brought them three drinks exactly the same as they had previously had.

"We have another magician here, Mr. Date," Lorraine joked, "A mind reader," and she thanked the young waiter and would have given him a large tip had the drinks not been free.

"I am continually amazed. We are having the best time of our lives. Aren't we, Anita?" Date squeezed Anita's hand.

"You got that right, I want to stay here forever." Anita replied and squeezed Date's hand back.

Seeing Parker sitting with a group of familiar people, Lorraine thought it might be best if she went over and asked him to join them. She didn't want to compete with Tia all night. Parker was totally thrown off balance but was glad she came over to him. See... The ice broke all by itself, he thought. He was a bundle of nerves though. When Lorraine got hold of his hand, the trepidation went away. Like a mother with her child, she lead him back to her table. Instantly, that feeling in his body started up again. His mind turned to mush. When he pulled the chair out for her and brushed against her dress, he felt fire on his fingertips. When he sat down, he thought he was sitting on a cloud, cloud number nine. When she spoke to him, he thought the birds of paradise were singing.

To Parker, the emcee's words turned into an indistinguishable hum. There was no light in the room only a blur before his eyes; and his olfactory senses registered nothing but

143

Lorraine's sweet perfume. If this was a dream, he didn't want to wake up. If this was reality, he didn't want to move or disturb it. And, if this was death, he wished it would last for an eternity. When the band started up and Lorraine asked him to dance, he could hardly get up. In his heart, he was convinced she felt something for him. But what? Pity perhaps.

Lorraine felt as though there was something terribly wrong and asked, "Are you okay?" Parker suddenly thought maybe there was something really wrong with him after all. Or maybe it was just a backlash from his hangover. It was now or never. He had to come to his senses and he stuttered, "Yes, yes, Lorraine, I am okay but am
overwhelmed with you. I am overwhelmed with your touch and with your entire being. Forgive me. I don't even know what I'm saying. I... I ... I have waited all my life for this moment, the moment to be alone with you, to see your beautiful face, to hear your heavenly voice."

Lorraine was in total shock. What was he talking about? They are no more alone now than they had been at the entry hall coffee table or at the casino...

"Can you? Will you come with me to my apartment, please? I promise I won't do anything to hurt you. You are the purpose of my life. Please come with me. We will come back, I just need to tell you something that I have had locked up inside me for so long, for decades. I will bring you right back. Please Lorraine! I need to explain something to you."

Whatever he needed to tell her, she felt responsible for everything. She felt no fear. She had to go with him. That was the least she could do. Without hesitation, she agreed.

The short ride in the elevator up to Parker's penthouse seemed like an eternity. She had no idea what he was getting at. Yet, something, something about him, maybe his voice, sounded so familiar. Lorraine was recalling him saying he had waited all his life for this moment... the touch of her hand... what is this? Where did he know her from? The purpose of his life. Those were pretty serious words.

They arrived at Parker's floor and the elevator stopped. The brushed stainless steel door slid open automatically and they stepped into a spacious living room furnished with stylish and expensive chattels. The curtains were drawn and soft music filtered though hidden speakers. There was a widescreen TV flanked by curtains and in full view along one of the walls was a computer equipped with a video camera and recording devices.

A bar jutted out from the corner and curved slightly, forming a semi-circle in front of a large mirror. The floor was covered in a light brown carpet that felt like mink. The air circulated gently, bringing with it the fragrance of an island populated with sweet smelling tropical flowers. The design and hue of the wallcoverings were programmed to change so slowly that it was almost unnoticeable to the eye. The framed pictures on the walls were not numerous, but outrageously expensive. They included Monet's 'Haystacks, at two different times of the day', his 'Red Boats', and Pablo Picasso's 'Three Dancers'. A voice-activated robot arm prepared two drinks. A Black Russian for Lorraine and coke and ice for Parker and placed them on a green granite counter top that had been cut from a fossilized prehistoric tree.

Secretly watching what was happening in Parker's apartment, Phillips was a little embarrassed. But he was also relieved to see that Parker was sticking to the rule of no alcohol.

Phillips locked his door so that no one could surprise him while he was watching the 'show' in Parker's penthouse.

Lorraine was in total awe.

"Please sit down," Parker asked Lorraine in an almost inaudible tone. Lorraine sat down on a sofa that was made of the finest Afghan wool and had been purchased from the collection of Zack's, a renowned furniture dealer on Rodeo Drive in LA.

As Lorraine was coming out of her amazement, Parker was handing her a drink with one hand and holding his in the other. He sat down in front of her in a red leather chair that was large enough to hold a family of four.

145

She was getting a violent headache from all this bedazzlement. She was desperately trying to place Parker in her mind but to no avail. She had met hundreds of men through her employment and hundreds more through her travels in Canada and other places around the world. He didn't remind her of anyone in particular. Was he from her class in school. Mannen? No one. No one stood out in her mind.

Clearing his throat and in a tremulous voice Parker began to speak. "Does the name Hoffmann ring a bell with you?" He pulled up his shirt sleeve exposing his left arm. Several white scars were visible close together that resembled cigarette burns on human flesh.

"No! Oh my God! You're not Alexander Hoffmann, the person I went to school with, are you?"

"Yes I am."

"I am speechless. I don't know what to say. You don't look the same at all. You don't sound the same either."

"I don't look the same because of the countless surgeries I've had to my face. Remember the bad acne I had when I was a kid? It just got worse as I grew older. My whole face has been replaced, which of course altered my voice as well."

"I can't believe it. Alex...I used to call you Alex in the old days, right?"

"Yes and I, we, all called you mommy. Remember?"

"That's right... but... but... what happened? What is this abduction all about?"

"This is all my doing. I did this because of you. I didn't know how else to get near you to find out how you would react to me, as an adult. Deep in my heart I am still a child. I am a very wealthy man now, Lorraine. I am a billionaire. I can afford anything. I have everything but peace of mind. Ever since we were in school together, you were the only person that ever showed any compassion towards me. I grew up without a mother or a father..."

Phillips was so overwhelmed he rejected the blackmail idea. After hearing such a heart-wrenching story, he would have to be a heartless beast to follow through with blackmail... and that he wasn't. In fact, he was feeling badly for eavesdropping on Parker's private affairs. He turned off the headset and went into the kitchen to get something good to eat.

"But, but, you had a father, Alex!"

"He was my grandfather. My father and mother died when I was only two. My grandfather raised me. You were the only female that touched my arm or my hand, ever. I would have died for your touch. You have no idea what it was like growing up without a mother. I used to lie in bed night after night craving for your touch, Lorraine."

Lorraine was totally flabbergasted. She had no idea what to say or what to do. "This is astonishing, Alex. So, why do you have me here? What do you want from me?"

"I am too afraid to ask you for anything. I would understand if you felt revulsion towards me. Perhaps you think I'm crazy or worse, a psychopath?"

"No, no, Alex, I don't think you're crazy and certainly you're not a psychopath. I think you're a very courageous person, coming out and telling me all this. You're a good man, Alex."

Lorraine's mind was racing between her school years and the present. What had she thought of him way back then? Had she felt pity for him then? Right now she was certainly feeling sorry for him. She felt as though she wanted to help him overcome his insecurities and help him out of his shell. Lorraine had a sense of all the pain and suffering he must have endured over the years... and was still suffering. He was tormented by the demons of his past. Lorraine felt total empathy. It must have been hard growing up without motherly love. And now, despite all his wealth, what he needed the most, he did not have.

"You have no idea what I've been through over the past twenty some years. You were on my mind first thing in the morning and last thing at night. And now, here you are. I am so overwhelmed that I don't know what to say and don't know what to do. But, I can tell you, I feel very at peace. I feel warm all over. I feel secure. I feel as though I have arrived back home after being away a million years. I feel like I've been reborn and nothing else matters. The pain isn't there anymore. I feel as if I could carry you in the palm of my hand and hold you up high for everyone to see. I could dance, shake hands with strangers and tell them that you are here. I could go to the end of the world and come back knowing you are here." Parker's voice was breaking as he spoke these words. His thoughts were flooding in and he finally gasped out the love that swelled inside him.

Lorraine was thinking that she had never heard words like these before, not even remotely close. Was he infatuated with her? Was he being honest? He must be honest. No one could think up something so bizarre or as wild as this. If he was on the level, he must have lived through hell. So now what? What is he going to do? What is she going to do?

She got up and held onto Parker's arm and he started to sob. He took Lorraine's hand and kissed it thanking her all the while.

"Poor Alex, my poor Alex! You waited all this time just to talk to me?" she said as she stroked Parker's face.

"Do you know how many times I had planned to call you on the telephone with some cockamamie idea but was afraid you'd ridicule me because you would have remembered all the awful things I used to do in school. But I did them just for you. I wanted to get your attention. I wanted you to touch my hand or my arm like a mother would. Like you're doing now. If you would have rejected me, I..., I, would have died. In order to get you out of my mind, I went to university and studied very hard. I majored in some very complicated sciences. I innovated and invented new technologies. I made some good investments that earned me a lot of money. Through my business, I thought maybe somehow somewhere I would meet you, get to know you. But in the back of my mind I was always afraid of rejection. Do you believe me, Lorraine?"

"Yes, yes, I believe you, Alex. But now you have to help me out too. I must get word to my boyfriend or else he will never forgive me. Let me call him. I'll be very brief. Then we will talk some more."

"Sure, use this phone," Parker replied and handed Lorraine a corded phone.

She dialled McCall's number and because he wasn't in, she left him a message saying she was fine. She felt that would make him feel relieved once he got home.

"Well, Mr. Parker or Mr. Hoffmann or Alex, where do we go from here?" Lorraine asked, as she sat back down on the sofa.

"Well, for starters, my legal name is Parker now. I changed my name a long time ago. I needed an English sounding name. In business it is better to have a good name. As our new bank manager, in public please call me Parker or Charles and in private you can call me anything you like. You have known me long enough."

Parker was ecstatic that Lorraine hadn't made fun of him. His headache disappeared and he was looking forward to the rest of the evening. He could fly like a bird now, soar like an eagle. Finally he was free. Finally free of his big inhibition, he became a completely changed man.

"Well, alright then, I'll call you Mr. Parker, Alex. And yes, you did promise me a job in your bank. You want me to be your bank manager, right? And this offer is still on the table, right?"

"It certainly is. I'll need your input on this . We can have a private bank of some sort, or a credit union, anything. We'll figure that out later. For the time being please carry on with the current duties you are doing at your bank. We'll be in touch. And now, I think we'd better go down and do some socializing or else people might think we've eloped."

CHAPTER 18

S omething had to give, McCall thought as he closed the door
behind him. Saturday had come and gone and there's still
no word from anyone. The bus and the hostages had to be
in a building somewhere. Otherwise the vehicle would have been
detected on Friday. You can't just hide thirty people in a shed.
They must still be in the bus. Or if they aren't, they had to be
locked up in a facility that had washrooms and sleeping quarters.
They had to be fed and attended to or locked in rooms or chained
or handcuffed to something. The place had to be big enough to
hide a bus. There had to be several people involved to watch over
the hostages day and night. There had to be guns or explosives or
other harmful devices to keep them under control. So...in the
morning we'll have to look at unoccupied factories, farms, mines
quarries, maybe even the old train station in Brantford. Wouldn't
it be something if the hostages were still in Brantford? Maybe at
the old Cockshutt building? Motels...hotels. Where did Lorraine
call from... Is she one of the abducted passengers? How could she
be? She never travelled by train. This is total craziness.

He turned on the TV and it was on CNN. The moderator
was talking about Donald Trumph and next year's elections in
the US. He switched to CBC. There the anchor lady was talking
about election results in Canada. He turned the TV off, undressed
and set the alarm to ring at seven and took a sleeping pill. The

time was quarter after one, Sunday morning.

　　As he closed his eyes, Hoffmann appeared again. McCall drew his gun and, in his dream, shot him. That was the end of Hoffmann. Next he imagined his pillow was Lorraine. He started hugging it and drifted off into a deep drug-induced sleep.

CHAPTER 19

"We thought you two might have left for the night," Date said laughing when Parker and Lorraine returned to their table.

"It's all business, Mr. Date," Lorraine said without blinking an eye and grinning widely.

"How's the band doing, Mr. Date?" she asked.

"I just wish I was twenty years younger. I'd show them." Date said and Anita cut in,

"Don't let him fool you. There might be snow on the mountain but there are still wild horses in the valley."

Everyone laughed, but Date was holding his side. And with a painful expression he lamented, "I might need crutches to walk with tomorrow. Do you have any crutches here, Mr. Parker?"

"We have some wheelchairs. We'll look after you Mr. Date, just dance your heart out," Parker said grinning boldly as he took Lorraine's hand and led her to the dance floor. The band was playing a slow dance. He was comfortable with that now.

The photographers were busy in the room, snapping pictures of everyone, including him and Lorraine. He felt a lot better. His headache was cured. In fact when he was holding Lorraine's hand, there was that strange sensual feeling again. Shivers ran up and down his spine and the rubber legs returned once more. It was a tango, a dance he could do without too much problem. However the next dance was a fast one. All he had to do was remember his dream of last night. He was good at it then. It was easier to think it than to do. He suffered through the dance, just basically standing and moving a little to the rhythm. He was happy when it ended and he could sit down. The dance made him sweat but not Lorraine, she had just got started and was looking more beautiful than ever.

The two 'movie stars' appeared to be bombed to those that recognized what bombed persons looked like. To those that didn't, they appeared lewd and inebriated. Everyone was rock-and-rolling and having a stellar time.

Just before the next dance began, Lorraine's number was drawn and she won a mountain bike.

"All I need now is a mountain," she said.

"You've got one of those too," Parker said and appeared to be joking, however he meant it. Parker owned a mountain too. The one just outside the resort.

"That's great Mr. Parker. During my lunch breaks I can do a little mountain biking. I have to exercise you know, and when I am finished I'll loan it to you."

Everyone laughed. Parker remembered he had promised Phillips' wife a dance. He excused himself.

Lorraine's head was buzzing. Something was happening to her that she couldn't place. Her thoughts of McCall and Parker were clashing. Here was Parker full of genuine love and desire and here was McCall with only one thing on his mind - sex. But McCall had other values too. He was good at sports and was handy at doing other things. He had a very good job with a very good salary. In Lorraine's mind, he only had one strike against him, but that was a major one. He seemed to like it the way it was; he liked to be single, free of responsibilities and couldn't see himself being tied down, even with her.

While dancing with Phillips' wife, Parker felt at peace with himself. All his inhibitions had left him. He had gotten along with Lorraine amazingly well, too well, maybe. She seemed to have a genuine compassion for him. She accepted him as a friend or maybe more than just a friend. She cared. She really felt for him. He touched his face where she had stroked him. The spot burned like a torch.

On his way back to their table he was thinking whether or not he should ask her to come back with him at the end of the evening and talk some more? No! Let's not push the matter he concluded. He was satisfied with his achievements for the night and decided to give it a rest, or what... but, he couldn't decide. After the dance with Phillips' wife, Parker rushed back to Lorraine's side.

He then thought about Date. What a pleasant, perceptive person! He had a job picked out for him already, but kept it to himself. Anita felt very lucky to have met such a good man as well. She held his hand all night, like lovers do.

The night was winding down. Some people had already left and Lorraine was feeling the effects of the excessive drinking. All that swimming and the sun and the dancing was more than she was used to. Because Date and Anita had already left, she asked Parker to see her to her room. She kissed him on the cheek and with "see you in the morning, Alex," she was about to enter her room when Parker mustered enough courage to hold onto her hand and squeeze it gently.

"Don't leave me Lorraine. Come with me I want to hear your voice. I want to be alone with you and tell you how I feel about you. I want to pour out my heart to you, all the beautiful thoughts I have stored up for you over the years. Please, Lorraine come up with me!" Lorraine didn't know whether she had heard Parker correctly or not.

She hesitated for a moment, just long enough to make him say it again, "Please, Lorraine, come with me. I... I want to tell you something... something very important to me. I mean well, I... I just need to talk to you in private."

Lorraine knew all along that she would go up with him,

only she didn't know what lay ahead. The position at his bank didn't seem that crucial or important or personal. Or was this the alcohol talking. He was drinking coke... She never expected to be hired for a job with such fanfare. Was Parker a predator? One way to find out. She made up her mind and said,

"Okay, Alex, I'll go up with you."

~

This time the elevator ride seemed shorter, perhaps because Parker was holding her hand. Or perhaps the suspense was overbearing. Perhaps the alcohol was affecting her senses. But one thing she knew, Parker made her feel good. For the first time in the evening she felt at ease with this man. She felt needed. Not just as an employee, but as a woman with strong inherent motherly qualities. Not only as a sex object, but as a person with feelings, understanding, and emotions. She felt pleased that she in some small way could help this driven person, who was real and in dire need of compassion.

The elevator door opened automatically once more. This time, Parker led Lorraine to a large couch and he sat down beside her. Lorraine put her hand on Parker's and looked him in the eye. Parker slid down off the couch onto his knees and pressed his face against Lorraine's legs. With a trembling voice he began,

"For twenty long years, I yearned for you as a child yearns for a mother. But tonight, you beautiful person, I yearn for you more than just as a child, I yearn for you as a man. I have a gift for you. You can accept it or refuse it. This used to be my mother's. I want to give it to you as a token of my genuine love." He presented Lorraine with a large sapphire ring.

"I know this is an unbelievable situation but now I know I have loved you all my life. From the moment you stepped off the bus I felt something no one else could feel. A feeling that confused me and scared me to death. I felt weak at the knees every time I touched you. My mind turned to pulp every time you spoke to me. It became obvious to me that I cannot live without you. You are my day; you are my night. There is nothing physical or imaginable out there that is more important to me than you."

Lorraine bent her head down next to his, and with her free hand she held his shoulder and for seconds or minutes or perhaps hours, they drifted together silently like two eagles in the sky making love and falling subconsciously towards earth until they knew to separate and fly freely in total satisfaction. Fly away, away to a destination that only the two of them could share.

"I know what's happened between us is right Alex, but it's not fair to do this to my boyfriend. It really is you that matters to me now. You are the person I deserve. You are a person with a love as great as the sky, a heart as great as the ocean. In this short period of time you have demonstrated more passion, more devotion and love to me than Chance did over all the years I spent with him. You are precious to me because you are genuine and honest. Your words come from your heart and I feel your sincerity in your touch. I accept this token of your love and I will stay with you as long as you want me. I will help you and be your mother and your lover and your guiding light in your turbulent sea." And she kissed him on his lips long and passionately.

She stood up and held his hand until he got up and then she lead him to his bedroom. There she took off all her clothes and she helped with his. The two fell into the bed. Knowing that he'd never slept with a woman before, Lorraine helped him to make love. It took only a few seconds but Lorraine felt satisfied and she knew that the next time it would be even better.

~

Later during that night, there were noises coming from the

156

pool where two guys and the two 'movie stars' were swimming and chasing after one another. They were all swimming naked, totally bombed out of their minds. It was a good thing everyone was too tired to notice because the scene might have started a small riot. Lorraine heard the noises because she was just coming from the bathroom. It didn't bother her. She fell back into Parker's bed and cuddled up to her new lover. In three seconds, she was asleep.

~

In the early hours of Sunday morning, two patrol cars were cruising up and down on regional road number five hoping to find the two dancers or the drug dealer. Each time they went by the resort, they saw a partially obscured bus in the parking lot and it started to look more and more curious. It was behind some trees and bushes, only one half of the rear end was visible.

At 6am, when the patrols decided to break for coffee, they stopped at Timmy's where Garret suggested to officer Mullen that she leave her car at the doughnut shop and the two of them drive up to the Eagle Hills Resort in his cruiser to take a closer look at the bus. Mullen, of course, rejected the idea because she thought Garret wanted to get fresh with her and she wanted to have no part of that.

Garret on the other hand stressed to officer Mullen that he was a happily married man, and though she looked good to him, he had no aspirations towards any extramarital Olympics.

"Besides you have a gun," Garret said.

Officer Mullen agreed to go, but wanted to drive her own car, and wanted to call it a joint investigation. When they arrived back at the resort, they found the gate closed. The bus was there and it indeed look interesting.

"This could well be the place where the hostages are being kept," Mullen speculated. The place was big enough and had all the amenities hostages would ever require.

There were some numbers, perhaps the equipment numbers printed on the side of the bus, which they couldn't see with the naked eye. The distance was too great. They couldn't make out the numbers. They had another problem. Their shift ended at eight o'clock. If they went to get binoculars and drove back to the resort, it would be past their quitting time. Someone else would have had to continue their investigation unless they asked for overtime. If they were to stay on the case they might have had to stay there all morning and Mullen wasn't going to do that.

"I have a three year old and a five year old. My husband and I had planned to take them to the zoo this afternoon after I've had a couple of hours sleep," Mullen said.

"Yeah, you're right. They might want us to put up a perimeter and stay all day... I don't want to do that either. This could develop into something nasty. There could be violence... We don't even have proper training for hostage situations. Let's just report this and let the day shift handle it." Garret said.

"By the looks of things, that bus isn't going anywhere, " Mullen agreed.

~

At quarter after eight in the morning, Garret and Mullen reported the sighting to their supervisor, who noted the event. He in turn instructed two patrols to go to the resort with binoculars and check out the bus. The binoculars were at the police station and by the time the officers got there plus had stopped for their coffee, it was quarter to eleven when they arrived at the resort. Since the gate was not open, they had to find a gap between the bushes to be able to see the partial numbers. The first three of the equipment numbers matched. They reported their find and waited for further instruction. The supervisor called Chief Hudson who wasn't home. He was at his cottage. Through a poor connection they spoke and decided to call the Emergency Task Force (ETF) right off the bat. The supervisor also called McCall at his office in Hamilton. The time was almost 11am.

~

McCall phoned Chief Stewart immediately and told him what was happening.

"Let Toronto handle this," Stewart said. That was a budget decision.

"Get everyone off the street and into the conference room and tell them to be ready. Just let them hang around... for whatever. They might need us, although I doubt it. The ETF guys are good and they probably won't need us at all."

CHAPTER 20

T he faint laughter outside and down the hall was defused by the curtains in the windows. The muffled sounds of the hustle and bustle downstairs reminded Lorraine of people moving in or out of her apartment building in St. Thomas. Suddenly, she came to realize that she wasn't in St. Thomas but at Eagle Hills Resort in Parker's bed. Reality started to hit home and ring its tiny bell. The bell ringer was saying hello, hello. And it wasn't a greeting hello, it was a wakeup call in many ways. Things happened too fast last night... perhaps. Was she unfair to Chance? Was she angry at Chance? No, but she was tired of the endless inaction on his part and the scale had tipped in Parker's direction. She hadn't realized she could do such a thing to Chance, and do it so suddenly. Was she drunk... no! Is she a gold-digger... no! Was she sorry this happened, no. She had been a tamed animal that had been kept by her handler until the built up frustration inside her spilled out and freed her. She closed her eyes and she heard Parker saying very serious things about love, affection and devotion to her. He said those words in the gentlest tone yet they were so powerful that even now they gave her goose bumps, and made her whole body tremble. The words he had said echoed in her mind. Was it only a dream? She was now feeling the meaning of those passionate and powerful words. She was rolling them over, examining them, sorting them, evaluating them and accepting them.

Step by step, she started to retrace the night's events. She felt no guilt, no remorse, no regret. She went into the elaborate bathroom almost losing her way around the different amenities. While she was turning and twisting on various knobs and faucets, Parker came in feeling a bit unstable and unsure of himself. Distantly, he remembered yesterday afternoon and doing something in here. But then, Lorraine took hold of his hand and drew him close to her body and kissed him affectionately. Feeling encouraged, he hugged her and became aroused instantly. They made love standing in the shower. Parker felt a lot more capable and was beginning to enjoy the kind of relationship he never knew existed.

He let water into the Jacuzzi and the two of them climbed in. The splashing and the enjoyment of one another resulted in more sexual activities until they decided it was time for some food. Parker ordered breakfast and the two sat down at the table. But before Lorraine sat down, she asked Parker for a robe. Parker went and got her one. A sharp pain flashed through his entire body. He dismissed it.

"Now comes the reality that we have to own up to." Lorraine said as she leaned over and kissed him on the cheek. Then she sat down opposite him.

"I'll be very busy this morning, but I meant every word I said to you last night. I love you. We are both savvy business people and you know that everyone's going home today. They'll all be gone before ten. I would like you to stay until I get a call from Phillips, this afternoon, then you can go too. You're going to McCall's apartment, I presume?"

"Yes. Chance and I will have to sit down and have a talk. And I'll be doing most of the talking. That's the only way I can do this. I'll go to his apartment today and tell him I am turning a new page. I have survived without him during these three days. In fact I enjoyed myself tremendously. I was offered a good position at a new bank. End of story."

"Can you do that, Lorraine?"

"Ah ha." Lorraine said, determinedly and with authority and without blinking an eye.

"He is not going to believe it, but I'll tell him he has to believe it. I don't even want to get into any details with him. I waited for years for his proposal to no avail. This time it's over. Time's up."

CHAPTER 21

Sunday morning McCall turned off his alarm clock that sounded like a jackhammer. It was a terrible way to wake up on any morning, not just for him but for anyone with responsibilities like his. On the other hand, had it gone off like a lullaby, he would have just rolled over and gone back to sleep.

~

Responsibilities started to punch him in the head, the second he stepped across the threshold of his office. Not gradually but all at once, his job landed on him like a wet blanket. The job would have been bad enough to cope with in his original function, but now looked very different since he was in charge. He had no idea what was coming. If he thought the hostage situation was bad, he wasn't facing reality. With a sour taste in his mouth he finished his coffee.

He received a call from Hudson's office and got hold of Chief Stewart right away to discuss who was going to handle the negotiations, if there were going to be any. The logical answer was McCall himself, of course, but it turned out the chief wanted the Toronto OPP to provide the manpower, and that included the negotiator. He emphasized the budget again. McCall had to hand it to the chief. He was on the ball.

Here he was, not even sworn in as the Deputy yet, and he might be negotiating with abductors already.

~

Lorraine went downstairs to her room and collected her belongings and took the elevator back to the penthouse. The door's electronic sensor recognized her right away and opened automatically. Parker was on his computer, clicking away on the keyboard, making notes about some nanotechnology.

"You're back already, I'll be just a sec, I have to write this down before I forget it. I have ordered some more coffee and some smoked salmon," he said. All this while subconsciously rubbing his inflamed stomach. The poisonous Datura had started its evil.

"Oh great. Another cup of coffee wouldn't hurt." Lorraine said and went to a mirror to check her hair. Finding it okay and seeing Parker up from the computer she smiled and asked, "How are you feeling this morning, Alex?"

"Oh, I am okay now, Lorraine, compared to yesterday... due to my misconstrued imagination and fear, I had a lot to drink. Much more than I've ever had. And all that booze did me in. I'm not an alcoholic. I just lost it. Phillips thought I was going to die and rushed me to the hospital."

Parker had no recollection of his bizarre actions at the penthouse. He merely thought he had had too much to drink. He didn't remember anything about the Sacred Datura or the trashing of his apartment. He thought he had gotten drunk and passed out. He thought Phillips had taken him to the hospital to sober him up.

He felt embarrassed about his over-indulgence. Yet on the other hand, he was relieved that his worries about Lorraine were unfounded. His 'wounds' were self inflicted. Even yesterday, even in his wildest dream, he'd never thought Lorraine would accept him as easily as she did. He thought she'd reject him. It had to be obvious to her that he was an honest man and that he was on the level. He was for real. When she put her hand on his left arm last night and squeezed it gently it, felt exactly the same as it did twenty years ago at the window at school, after he had burned blisters on it. Last night he took her hand and kissed it.

"... I want to tell you what we are doing today, Lorraine. I have instructed Phillips to follow every step precisely the way I planned it. First and foremost, the authorities have to know that no one was harmed. Everything was a hoax. Everything was designed for the sake of publicity."

A buzzing noise came from the direction of the door and a waiter with a tray appeared on a small screen. Parker snapped his fingers and the door opened.

As he greeted the two, the waiter came in and set the tray on a coffee table. Parker returned the greeting.

"Is there anything else you need sir?... Ms. Wilkinson...?"

"No thank you, Stanford." Parker said.

Lorraine shook her head. Stanford left the room. Parker continued talking about his plan;

"The passengers are being taken home as we speak. We have several limousines that can handle six to eight people. They might even all be gone by now. And I have a driver to take the bus back to Simcoe. Once everyone has left, Phillips can take you to McCall's apartment and when you see him he'll have no idea where you have been these last three days, right?"

"That's right."

"When you go to his apartment, you can tell him anything and he'll believe you, right? You can tell him you were away on your bank's request."

"If I said that, I would be lying. I'd sooner tell him the truth. I'll tell him I was one of the abducted passengers. Otherwise it might become too complicated, Alex."

"Okay then. I like your decision. We'll send you to his place by limousine. You can tell him I have offered you a job as manager at the bank here at the resort and that you got twenty-five thousand dollars. You can tell him everyone else is offered employment and you can tell him about me."

"Let's not do that, Alex. I would sooner not say anything about you and me and that you're actually Alex Hoffmann. I'll simply tell him you're Charles Parker, the entrepreneur. I'll tell him you offered me the position and I accepted it. And I'll leave it at that. How does that sound?"

"That's good! My guess is he'll cheer for you."

"I hope so. Now, Alex... "

"What is it, Lorraine?"

"Oh never mind, it's not important. I'll just do it the way we discussed. That way Chance will be on our side and will say the right things to his chief. He'll ask me some dicey questions but I'll handle them as we go along. And, I'll definitely let you know how the police are planning to handle this situation."

"But, what was it that you were going to say?"

"A time line. The bank will need time to replace me."

"Give them all the time they need. I haven't even decided what bank I want. I will need your input on that choice. This will be an amicable separation. We might even want to use your bank?"

"That's great, Alex."

"You are an angel, Lorraine." Parker said and if he were a bird he would have started flying around the room.

CHAPTER 22

The ETF unit was mobilized and arrived at the resort at 11:53am and precisely fifteen minutes before Lorraine's limousine arrived at McCall's apartment. At noon, McCall's phone rang at the headquarters and the desk sergeant said the caller, a Max Phillips from Eagle Hills Resort, wanted to talk to the person in charge.

Phillips thought he would get the chief on the line but McCall told him he was in charge. Phillips stated that the abduction was a hoax and that it had been done as a publicity stunt. McCall was astounded. He didn't know what to say. He was speechless. He felt as though someone had hit him on the head and let all the blood out of his body. He felt as though his brains had been replaced by fog. His mouth became dry and his tongue felt like sandpaper and it didn't fit his mouth. His mouth stayed open all the time Phillips was talking. Since McCall didn't answer, Phillips thought perhaps he had fainted. He repeatedly asked, "Are you there?"

Yes, he was there alright. He thanked Phillips for the information and hung up. He hadn't even organized his men yet. Everybody was waiting for him in the conference room. He felt dizzy. At first he had thought the guy was just joking. But he had to believe him because he said there was no one left at the resort, even the bus had been returned to its owner.

How was he going to explain this to his chief? This is an

unprecedented nihilism. This Parker guy has to be one sick puppy. The whole world had been turned upside down for nothing - for publicity. The whole thing had been a hoax. And he felt as though he had been duped and they had all been victimized.

The chief is going to die when he hears this, McCall thought. He feared that this was an absolute 'Keystone Cops' scenario. But it had certainly turned out better than a real abduction would have.

For the longest time, McCall sat frozen in his new armchair. Then the phone shrilled brutally. The secretary said his girlfriend Lorraine was on the line.

He was about to tell her that the abduction issue was over, when Lorraine stated that she had been one of the abducted passengers on the bus. She was calling him from his apartment. She said, this 'Mystery Bus' affair had been a publicity stunt for the Eagle Hills Resort and that she had been offered a bank managerial job at the resort. McCall continued to be dumbfounded. He managed to stammer out that he was coming home momentarily... once he had explained everything to his chief. Lorraine told him to take his time.

The fact that Lorraine was going to be the bank manager at this new resort got McCall thinking. He had to start looking at how to support her in this new position. He needed some time to mull things over.

~

In the meantime the ETF unit arrived at the resort surrounded the whole are. The gate keeper was having fits trying to figure out what was happening. He had wanted to call Phillips but the ETF wouldn't let him use the phone. In fact he was under arrest. Then the empty bus came rolling down the driveway, with its original license plate, being driven by a uniformed driver in a uniform hat. There were a dozen guns aimed at it and a bull horn was blasting the driver to stop.

Finally, luckily, McCall got hold of the ETF captain and

168

told him to drop everything. He told him to call off his men because all the passengers had been taken home and this whole thing had been a hoax. The ETF captain blew up and began calling Parker bad names, accusing him of starting this whole sordid affair. McCall was thinking along the same lines too.

The ETF captain was so riled that he told McCall he could shove this case and deal with the media himself since he had been involved with this mess from the start. McCall replied that he would.

Suddenly, McCall felt very lonely, as if he was in an empty room, with no windows and no doors.

He couldn't just say to his officers "Sorry, guys. This was a hoax and it is all over." He had to think. First, he called Lorraine back and told her he'd be tied up at the office for a while. Then he phoned the chief at home and in so many words explained the situation to him. He shocked Chief Stewart. Stewart thought this Parker guy must be absolutely crazy. He indicated something about Parker needing a good lawyer and a psychiatrist. And that he didn't know which one Parker needed first.

What could McCall do? He agreed with the chief. Stewart had said to go ahead with the report, but he wanted to see it before it was given to the press. McCall had no problem with this request.

The chief said he wanted to see Parker at the station and that he was coming right in. He wanted Parker brought in and wanted him on the carpet. Stewart was concerned about the police image. He had a point. McCall too was greatly concerned about the department's image. However, McCall found out that Parker was not available and Phillips was representing the resort. Since he had already spoken to Phillips, he called the chief back and asked him if he wanted to talk to Phillips. Stewart said he did.

"Bring him in!" he said very firmly and clearly, without a cigar in his mouth.

Once they had Phillips in the office and had heard his extraordinary story, they let him go home and the two of them just sat at the table dumbfounded.

"Who is going to believe this crap," the chief asked.

"Nobody," McCall answered and told the chief he would handle the story.

The chief replied, "You go ahead," and said he was going home. McCall sat at his desk for ten minutes before he could come up with something worthwhile. Had it not been for the computer age, his wastepaper basket would have been overflowing with crumpled sheets of paper. Finally he cobbled together a statement. He didn't like it, but it was the true picture. He was about to call the chief's house when he appeared at his door with a two inch cigar stuffed in his mouth. Thank God it was only two inches, he thought. He figured it would only last for a few minutes. Although engulfed in that putrid smoke even for few minutes would still make him smell like smoked fish.

~

As the chief was reading McCall's report he was standing up making faces all the while. After he approved it, he tossed it onto his desk and sat down and crossed his arms looking at McCall like a father might look at his pregnant thirteen year old daughter... and said "What now?"

"Someone at the Eagle Hills Resort, will have to answer that question," McCall replied as cheerfully as he could as he slid his press write-up back for the chief to sign.

PRESS RELEASE.

"On Friday evening, thirty people were abducted from a decommissioned railroad station in Brantford, Ontario.

Fearing the worst, police forces throughout Ontario were mobilized to look for the bus with the abducted passengers. The bus could not be found and there was no ransom demand made by the abductors. Today, a couple of sharp eyed OPP officers found the 'Mystery Bus' hidden at the Eagle Hills Resort. Plans were quickly made to free the hostages. When police arrived at the resort, it was found that all the passengers had already been taken home by the abductors. It appears that this whole incredible fiasco was a hoax, designed to promote the new resort.

While it is obscure as to who is responsible for the hoax, it is absolutely clear that the person or persons in charge will be prosecuted to the fullest extent of the law.

Even though the chief wasn't enthralled, he accepted McCall's write up as it was.

"Short and sweet. Let's go with it, McCall. Have one of the girls print this up on our letterhead and fax it to all of our units including CP (Canadian Press). You can sign it or I can. It doesn't matter. This guy either has too much money or he is totally crazy. Either way the government is not going to be very happy with Parker. Then there's the press. It will be interesting to see what they will make of it. No doubt, they will turn the story inside out, giving even more publicity to the resort. This will be a media circus. But all in all, this is one hell of a burden off my back," the chief said.

McCall felt the same way, and immediately thought about his vacation. He could do what he had set out to do after all.

He wiped his forehead and subconsciously sucked in several cubic feet of Chief Stewart's second hand cigar fumes. The smoke made him dizzy and he wanted to throw up. Instead he took it like a man, thinking that by the time he came back from his vacation, the chief would have announced his retirement and he would be out of there...and no more pollution.

He called the WRL, Rutherford's office and Marcel Lefebvre, then decided to go home. He thought about his vacation again and figured by the time they got back everything would have fizzled out.

After he parked his car in his garage, as he usually did, he walked by the drugstore. The druggist, who had gotten to know him by now, stopped him at his door and started talking. He asked

McCall about the TH&B affair and McCall told him it was over. He asked McCall if he had solved the case. McCall lied and told him that he had. The druggist thought McCall should get a badge for working on it day and night.

"By the way, what's your name?" the pharmacist asked.

"Chance McCall."

"Chance...? How you spell that?"

"The same way you spell chance, like in I've got a good chance."

"Who gave you that name?"

"I would guess my parents did. In any case I didn't have a chance to argue about it. I was too young when I was born."

"I like that name and I'll name my child that when it's born," he said.

"What if it's a girl?" McCall asked.

"That's okay. I'll name her Chance too."

McCall thanked him for that and he knew he had a friend for life. He went upstairs.

CHAPTER 23

That Sunday afternoon the WRL office was buzzing. The excitement was 11 on a scale of 1 to 10. Since this was the weekend there were very few high officials around. Text messages and phone calls were flying back and forth between ministry officials on golf courses and justices in cottages, and emotions were running high. Cool heads did not prevail. Everyone smelled blood and wanted to sue the resort until some high-powered lawyers straightened the story out. The lawyers knew the OPP wouldn't say much about anything because they had to put this thing through their internal ringer first.

The lawyers were looking at the facts, and the intent. Was the intent criminal? Obviously not. The intent appeared to be motivated by one reason only - publicity. The law is not very strong in the area of obnoxiousness. Was any damage done? Obviously the damage was minimal. Was anybody hurt? No one was hurt. In fact, a lot of people benefited greatly. Did anybody complain? No one complained. Therefore, there was no cause for a charge. The best scenario was to set a price for fixing the tab on the tracks, and perhaps some other material costs, and try to sue for that. The court costs would definitely outweigh the bother.

"We can't forget that with each move there's publicity involved," one of the lawyers warned. "Good publicity for the resort. No publicity for anyone else."

Finally, the lawyers suggested an amicable get together

and an agreement on some kind of donation to some charities. That took the wind out of all animosities towards the resort.

Later on, when McCall read the summary from the lawyers, he did smell a Keystone Cops scenario. That did not make him happy.

The papers didn't make too much fuss either because they didn't want to promote the resort free gratis.

Everyone saw through the sham, just like he did, in hindsight.

CHAPTER 24

When McCall opened the door to his apartment, Lorraine was on the phone. He didn't want to bother her because it sounded like business. She was finished with her conversation shortly and they hugged. He found her a little tense.

They sat down at the kitchen table and she apologized for not calling him sooner than she did.

He told her he understood and that he figured she was in that covert operation with the bank. She stopped him and told him she was one of the abducted persons on the 'Mystery Bus' and that everyone was paid $25,000 for keeping silent until today. He replied that for that kind of money he would have kept silent too.

"But, then you left a message for me on Saturday evening," he said.

"Yes, because they let me call you. I am special. I am going to be the bank manager there," Lorraine said in an official cold voice.

"Isn't that cool, and I'm going to be the deputy chief," he said to Lorraine. He told her that Frank Adams had died and he would likely be promoted to that position. It wasn't for sure yet, but almost 99% sure. Better yet, McCall said,

"I might even become the chief." But he knew he was probably reaching a little bit with that.

McCall suddenly started to feel like a stranger in his own apartment. His words sounded hollow, as if someone else was speaking them and he was listening. His words seemed to bounce off the walls and back at him.

They sat by the table for hours it seemed and she told him what had happened from the beginning. McCall was quite suspicious about the chain of events. The stolen battery, the WRL leaflet, the fake derailment and the bus transfer. They all seemed to come together perfectly in the end. To him, a seasoned police officer, something seemed odd. Something didn't seem to pass the proverbial 'smell test'.

He could understand the phony derailment and the transfer bus, but the stolen battery and the WRL flyer appeared to be a little too bizarre. He had to think about that.

She told him about the STORES and the food and the Wilsons being there, and then of course about the Bay Street Boys. McCall felt a little jealous and wished he had been there. McCall noticed Lorraine seemed to be somewhat aloof as she spoke. It might have been her excitement about the stellar job at this new bank.

McCall started talking about the consequences, that Parker had to face. It appeared she wasn't too worried about anything. She said Parker's company had lots of money and this affair was part of a promotion of the resort. McCall grimaced and just left it at that. He should have commented, but what the hell...it was none of his business.

McCall suggested they go out for dinner and Lorraine agreed. But out of the blue she said "I'm leaving you, Chance."

McCall couldn't have been more stupefied if the chief had appeared in front of him bare naked.

He said, "What?"

She said it again. "I'm leaving you, Chance."

He wanted to get up from the table and walk back and forth in front of her, but he couldn't. He felt paralyzed. "How in hell did this come about?" he asked.

"Simple. I found out that I could manage just fine on my own. I haven't been without you anywhere for the last five years. When I went somewhere I always went with you. You were always there. You must remember the times I hinted about an engagement ring... and you said some stupid thing about the size of the diamond. Do you remember, Chance?"

"I was just joking. I didn't think you were serious about getting a ring."

"I wasn't just serious about a ring. I was hoping you'd propose to me, Chance. My poor father would have liked to see his only daughter married and my mother would have too. You see, Chance... I, I can't tell you to grow up. I mean, a woman hasn't all the time in the world to have a family. And obviously you aren't thinking of a family. You always had your fun with the guys, and your cards and that... I am not going on a vacation with you. I am done as we speak. If you want to go for dinner, that's fine with me, I'll go with you. I'll even pay half. But that's it. As a couple, we're done."

McCall was so shocked, he felt nauseated and devastated.

He felt as though his world had collapsed right in front of his eyes. He wanted to say that he'd call a taxi, and she could leave right now, but then she would have just walked out the door, kissed him goodbye and he would never see her again. Instead he said, "Is the Air Port okay with you for dinner?"

"I guess," Lorraine said.

"Let's go then. Oh, you can pay half if you want to. You can afford it now. There's got to be more to this story. We're not going to throw five years of our lives out the window, just like that. And I am not counting the years we spent together in school."

They sat in McCall's car.

Lorraine began to feel uneasy. She knew where he was coming from and knew where he was going but knew she had to stand her ground.

At the Air Port, McCall parked his car and together they headed towards the entrance. The place was peaceful this time.

When they arrived inside, he got a standing ovation which he never expected. The patrons cheered him for solving the abduction case without firing a shot.

"I didn't come here for this, Lorraine. I hope you can understand that."

She knew McCall was known here, but she didn't want to be part of any celebration. She wished she hadn't come.

They went to the rear dining area.

"It would appear to me that a ring would have prevented this situation. I'll go and buy one tomorrow. A big one, and one for myself. If that's what you want, Lorraine. I'm not giving you up that easily."

They ordered their food.

Lorraine said nothing.

"Everyone knows we are a couple and they all know I care for you a lot. I almost went crazy looking for you. I phoned everybody I could think of."

For Lorraine, things were becoming a little more complicated than she had planned. She began to think that maybe McCall was going to ask some questions about Parker. How much am I going to tell him, if anything at all? But then again, he can find out everything about anybody... if he wants to. And he probably wants to. I cannot lie about Parker's identity. It must have been the booze... what did I say to Parker? Did I say, "You're the person I deserve. You're a person with love great as the sky...I feel the sincerity in your touch. I accept this token of your love... and I will stay with you as long as you want me." Did I say that? That sounds like a commitment. I am committed now, or am I? Is McCall being sincere or is he just putting this on?

The food came, and Lorraine started talking again;

"You see how fast things change. You would have just gone along the same way for the next twenty years had I not said something. You need me for a trophy, for people to see. But when you come here alone, nobody misses me. You don't need me at your card games, you don't need me when you go drinking with your buddies. You only need me sometimes. Once or twice a month... and I come running. I should have put my foot down long ago. It's not entirely your fault. It takes two to tango. However, it is now my decision to leave. Deep inside I don't feel loved, Chance. I feel nothing... You know, Chance... I don't feel anything right now. I feel that you're just reacting to what I said. Maybe because you're a cop... a tough guy, or you don't know how to express yourself, or maybe you're just an uncompassionate guy, too hardened, always reacting to problems or troubles or crimes or murders and that sort of thing."

Chance ordered a bottle of wine.

"Well, if we aren't going away together... what are you going to do?"

"I'll visit with my mom. I haven't seen her lately anyway."

"This is incredible. I can't believe this. Are you sure you want to do this, Lorraine?"

"Yea. I've made up my mind, Chance. I want you to take me to the resort and I'll drive myself home from there."

"But you have no car."

"They have lots of company cars there, I'll just take one of those."

"Well ...if that's what you want, Lorraine... You're breaking my heart, you know."

"It isn't easy for me either, Chance."

"Can I call you sometime?"

"Oh yeah. Call me, any time. We can still be friends."

McCall thought, 'We can still be friends' sounds like someone talking about the morgue. DOA. Holy shit... one disaster after the other.

"I'll pay for everything, Lorraine. Let's go then."

CHAPTER 25

A s the lawyers suggested, the OPP head honchos and the WRL had an amicable get-together at the Eagle Hills Resort with all expenses paid by Parker's company, of course. The key lawyers were there too, including Drew Bundy who had never gotten a penny out of the whole abduction affair.

He wasn't too upset though, because Parker and he were buddies and his stay at the resort was always free. Not only that, but he'd made millions on real estate deals Parker had cut him in on.

In fact, Bundy's three kids two girls and a boy and Parker's two boys had practically grown up at the Resort learning the ropes of the business from the earliest age.

When Parker married Lorraine, Bundy was Parker's best man. Their wedding at the Resort was so elaborate that the papers fought amongst themselves over who was going to cover the event.

The CP was there and some local papers. CBC and CNN wanted some cameras located on the premises but were refused. However the Resort had allowed a moderator Evan Solomon, formerly from the CBC and a person named Anderson Cooper to be there with an I-pod phone/camera. The security device which prevented transmission from the Resort was turned off. The food was provided by the same Hungarian chefs who had cooked on that memorable weekend in the summer.

The wedding gowns were made by Mrs. Toti of Port Dover, Ontario, whose daughter Sylvia and husband David Morrison had also been invited. Date and Anita were there too and they were expecting a child in the next year. Ecstasy Date became an aunt?

The two dancers had spent all their money within a month. They never came to work for Parker and therefore never received any shares in the company. In one year, shares went from one hundred dollars to one thousand dollars a share.

The wedding lasted two days and the newlyweds took an extended honeymoon to an exotic island in the Caribbean.

The following year, Parker completed his papers on the FUEL (Free Unlimited Energy from Lightning) project. He worked out the formula for the collection of the immense electric power available from lightning strikes and the mode of Temporary Power Retention (TPR). This power didn't need to be held for a length of time since it could be replenished immediately. This was possible because there were electrical storms all the time across the globe.

The mode of Wireless Power Transportation (WPT), is something Parker had already figured out at the same time he built the device to control radio wavelengths and microwaves for cell phones. However, he didn't make the announcement until the first FUEL collector/transformer was completed in a secret location in Nanticoke, Ontario.

Parker could hardly wait to see the oil producing nations scrambling to invest in his technology. The closure of the Oil Sands in Alberta made him happy. Overnight Parker became the richest and the most powerful man on earth but he didn't care about power, he only cared about Lorraine, his Mommy.

And just imagine. This all happened because his grandfather was resourceful enough to save the gold cuttings from his engraving business.

When Chief Stewart retired, shortly after the Mystery Bus affair, Chance McCall became the chief of police. His name was recorded in the history books right next to the most bizarre abduction in the world and history was kind to him, He wasn't likened to the Keystone Cops.

When McCall phoned Lorraine one evening, she was in the process of moving from St. Thomas to the resort. She was very reserved and didn't say much. McCall told her that he had found out who Parker actually was. After a long silence she said she wasn't surprised and that Parker was in the hospital recovering from some kind of poisoning. McCall thought to himself, he should have hit the son-of-the-bitch on the head and killed him down at the lake twenty years ago and gotten it over with. But he didn't tell Lorraine that. He just said, "Have a good life Lorraine," and hung up.

Parkers kidneys were shot and the doctors gave him six months to live, unless they found the right donor...

THE END

Persons in attendance were:

Chance McCall, police superintendent, co-protagonist
Lorraine Wilkinson, RCBC, co-protagonist
Dennis Stewart, chief of police
Margaret Stewart, chief's wife
Adam, Margaret's, younger brother
Lucas Wilson, magician/illusionist
Missy Wilson, wife and assistant to Lucas
John Edmonds, insurance business
Brad Smith, insurance business
Matthew Sommers, druggist
Dale, police corporal
Frank Adams, deputy chief
Max Phillips, security/ground manager
Dallas Mattison mngr.
Rutherford, police captain
Mike Pucci, detective
Peter Wilde, detective
Shelly, police clerk
Marcel Lefebvre, RCMP commissioner
Guy Dubois, sergeant
Hudson, Toronto OPP chief
Garret, OPP officer
Mullen female OPP officer
Drew Bundy, lawyer
Lincoln Alexander Hoffmann, B. Dec. 31/1970
          Aka Charles Parker and

El Sicko and
Alex, billionaire co-protagonist
Gerhard Hoffmann, Alex's grandfather
Adela, Gerhard's wife D. 1948
Joseph Hoffmann, Gerhard's son B. Nov.11/47- D. 1972
Judith, Joseph's wife D. 1972
Oscar Schindler, deceased 1974, industrialist,
as stated in Wikipedia.
Armstrong, teacher
Mannen, Alex's schoolmate
Ed Clement, retired station master
John Kleiner, conductor
William Bertling, train engineer
Stetson Skilling, WRL
Brendon, WRL
George Date, retired
George Date Jr., teacher
Roger Date, musician
Denise Date, Roger's wife
Ecstasy Date, Roger's daughter
Matthew Harai, master chef
Baird Jones, alert man walking his dog
Susan Crandall, receptionist

The passengers and their room numbers
01Seals, Andy
02Diab, Dave
03Robinson, Dave
04Matka, John
05Tank, Henry
06Kevin, Mike
07Gibson, George
08Christy, Lisa
09Kelly, Karen
10Jansen, Evan
11Taylor, Philburg

12Firman, George
13Everly, Zelda
14Mack, Adam
15Elder, Frank
16Varga, Imre
17Gilbert, Ben
18Thorne, Tiron
19Sinclair, Tia
20Sullivan, Dave
21Sullivan, Sara
22Markle, Net
23Markle, Diana
24Foreman, Zak
25Foreman, Irene
26Todd, Anita
27Klint, Stephan
28Livingstone, Cythia
29Wilkinson, Lorraine, as above, co-protagonist
30George Date
Mrs. Toti tailor extraordinaire, from 'Tusks of Terror' book
Sylvia & David Morrison from 'Tusks of Terror' book.

Heron Point Golf and Country Club is in Ancaster, Ontario, Canada. This land used to be a dairy farm where Charles Jambor worked as a hired man. When he arrived in Canada as a young man in 1957, he did not speak a word of English. For other works by Charles Jambor read "Kid Without Fear" an autobiography and "Tusks of Terror" a fictional novel.

Other recognisable places: The Province of Ontario, Canada, Cities of Brantford, Hamilton, St. Thomas &Toronto. HWY 403, Grey St. & Wayne Gretzky Blvd. in Brantford.

Charles Eric Jambor

www.ingramcontent.com/pod-product-compliance
Lightning Source LLC
Chambersburg PA
CBHW070026260626
47159CB00005B/1960